Her Death of Cold

HER DEATH OF COLD

by

Ralph McInerny

A FATHER DOWLING *Mystery*

THE VANGUARD PRESS
NEW YORK

Published by Vanguard Press, Inc., 424 Madison Avenue,
New York, New York 10017.
Published simultaneously in Canada by Gage Publishing Co.,
Agincourt, Ontario.

Library of Congress Catalogue Card Number: 76-39728
ISBN: 0-8149-0781-4
Designer: Tom Torre Bevans
Manufactured in the United States of America.

For Marvin O'Connell

Her Death of Cold

1

IT WAS three in the morning.

The sound of the ringing telephone reached down into the peaceful confusion of his dreams and drew him forth unwilling into wakefulness. The old voice spoke urgently in his ear. He closed his left eye and made out the time on the digital clock beside his bed. It was cold in the room because of the air conditioner, whose hum became audible as he thought of it. He assured Sylvia Lowry that she had nothing to fear.

"But I am afraid, Father. Terribly afraid."

"You mustn't be."

"I do not want to die."

"You are not going to die." His reassuring tone might have been meant to confer immortality upon her. "Everything is going to be all right."

"They all hate me. I've told you."

Although there was no moon, his room seemed bright. Dawn was not far away. Neither was impatience. He wondered if he would be able to coax sleep back again. Why was Sylvia whispering?

"They don't hate you, Sylvia."

He imagined the old woman, alone in her house, desperate with imaginary fears. Was she losing her mind? Had she already lost it? She said that her childrn hated her, but he wondered if they gave her that much thought. He had met the daughter, Sharon. On the whole, he preferred the troubled mother. Sylvia's fear, her doubts, gave her a claim on him. Even at this hour.

"Why are you calling now?"

"I can't sleep."

He pressed his eyes shut and sleep seemed to await him in the renewal of darkness. "Pray," he urged her. "Say your beads."

"I have every light in the house on."

"Good."

"It doesn't help."

He must be patient. She was an old woman, a wealthy old woman. Natural death could not be far off. Perhaps imagining the threat of violence was a way of domesticating death, an insistence that it was accidental, an unlooked for interruption, not the inevitable end in store for her and everyone. For himself as well.

"What can I do for you, Sylvia?"

"Nothing. I don't know. I had to hear the sound of a human voice."

"Perhaps your children . . ."

There was a dry laugh at the other end of the line. "They told me to stay away from you."

"Oh?"

"They resent your kindness to me."

Kindness? The word seemed an accusation. He felt that he showed her only a grudging patience. "Say your rosary, Sylvia. Ask God's protection."

"Thank you, Father."

After he had hung up the phone, Roger Dowling turned on his side and pulled the covers over his shoulder. He had not been much help to Sylvia. A feeling of inadequacy came over him, he had been no help at all. The realization did not stop his yawn. He pressed his eyes tightly closed and strange lights, subjective lightning without thunder, played upon his lids. The sound of the air conditioner grew, seemed irregular, took on worrisome rhythms. Father Dowling opened his eyes.

He had been told that the wiring of the rectory should be replaced. The roof too needed work. He could afford neither. A different worry brought him fully awake. Was he patient with Sylvia Lowry because of her money? God forbid. In an oblique, half-teasing way she had said she would be leaving money to the parish. Had she told her children that? Did they think he meant to exploit her piety?

He must have a talk with Sylvia, a serious talk, after the noon Mass that she faithfully attended. Her priest he must be, he wanted to be, but he would not be her beneficiary. He would speak to her daughter too, before Mass. Sylvia should not be living alone.

2

IF ROGER DOWLING lost some sleep because of Mrs. Lowry, her daughter, Sharon Cordwill, lost a golf match.

"Oh, no!" she had cried when Dowling went to see her. "At three in the morning! Father, I am so sorry."

She leaned toward him and put a hand on his arm, her tanned face a mask of concern. They stood in the driveway of the Cordwill home. It was not yet nine o'clock. Sharon was dressed for golf, navy blue skirt, white short-sleeved blouse, anklets. There was the look of the fairway in her eyes.

"Every day, if I can manage it," she answered when he asked how often she golfed.

Her skin was leathery from the sun, but aside from that, golf seemed to serve her like the fountain of youth. Roger Dowling thought ruefully that she could not be much younger than he was.

"Today is my eighteen-hole group. We are very serious."

Her eyes crinkled nicely when she smiled. From the street came the sound of a horn. Her ride was here.

"I'll tell them I can't go."

"Don't be silly. I just wanted to let you know." But he felt like a traitor to Sylvia, coming here.

"Three in the morning." She shook her head but her eyes were dragged to the waiting car. "Are you free later, Father?"

"I say a noon Mass."

"Have lunch with me. At the Fox River Country Club. Come at one."

The dining room they ate in seemed an extension of the golf course visible through its windows. The doors were flush with the practice putting surface immediately outside. There was a humous smell of mown grass, of roses, of all the hot and honied aromas of the Midwestern summer. Sharon was still in golf shoes, no problem on the cork floor, and her blonde hair was pulled back tightly on her head. She sipped her daiquiri, studying him.

"How was your game?" he asked.

"Don't ask. The heat was terrible." Her eyes met his directly. Lunch with a priest did not intimidate her. "Of course I kept thinking of mother." She spoke as if he had accused her of neglect. "She won't live with us, we can't move in with her, and she refuses to go to a nursing home. I don't blame her."

Her chin lifted and Dowling could see a bit of Sylvia in her daughter then. Sharon smiled a strange little smile.

"I suppose the least we could do is take out her phone. What on earth does she mean, she's afraid of us? Believe me, at three in the morning, my worst enemy is safe from me. Do you think her mind is going?"

"I've only known your mother a few months. In that time she hasn't changed."

"She likes you."

Of course that was impersonal. He was a priest; it was his office and function Sylvia respected, not he. Surely it wasn't necessary to point this out to Sharon.

"She likes you and she's afraid of us."

"What was she like?"

"When I was a girl?" Sharon tossed her head and the lock of hair returned to her forehead. She looked past Dowling, at the window, at the golf course, beyond, but he sensed that her glance was inward. "She was marvelous. Just marvelous. She was one of the shakers and movers here, I can tell you." Sharon looked around her with belligerent tenderness. "She had a seven handicap."

"Is she still a member?"

"Mother? Now? Heavens no."

"She got religion?"

"Oh, she always had it, I guess." Sharon seemed to expect some protest, but he did not oblige her. "I think it goes back to when she gave up golf. She wasn't all that older than I am now." Sharon looked at her hand, which she opened and closed. "Arthritis. She refused to settle for a duffer's game. She saw that it was affecting her grip and that it would only get worse, so she just put away her clubs and that was that."

"She stopped coming here?"

"Not while Dad was alive. This place was the center of his life."

"When did he die?"

Her eyes rose to the ceiling of acoustical squares. She might have been counting off the needed number. "Six years ago."

"Has there been talk of selling the house?"

"Good Lord, no. We don't want her to *sell* it. That is the *Lowry* house."

She made it sound like an ancestral castle. Roger Dowling suspected that the Lowry name still summed up for Sharon what was important in life. Was this club the center of her life too? Perhaps, like her maiden name, it was something mythic, more than itself, an outward sign of inward what? Style? Money? But money is a kind of style.

She said, "I'm going to have another of these. I don't suppose you want more tomato juice?"

"No."

"You realize everyone will think you're drinking Bloody Marys?"

"The best of both worlds."

But he felt he was getting the worst of both. However pitiful Sylvia's condition might appear, Roger Dowling found it preferable to her daughter's. Did Sharon know that sometime, eventually, without fail, her own turn would come? Arthritis, something worse or not so bad, but something to shatter the formidable self-assurance she had. And would she weather it even as well as her mother had? Father Dowling wished there were some way he might warn her, but of course there wasn't. He wondered if it wasn't her daughter's sophisticated innocence that frightened Sylvia Lowry.

When her drink had come, Sharon gave Dowling her theory as to why her mother feared her own children. He must not think the old woman simply made things up. They were indeed worried about her. She had never handled money while Mr. Lowry was alive and of late she had become increasingly eccentric where money was concerned.

"She feels threatened when we mention it. I suppose it must sound as though we're worried about our inheritance. Has she ever mentioned her will to you?"

"To me? Of course not."

His denial, technically true, sounded vehement, as if he meant to erase his early morning doubts rather than answer Sharon. Her expression told him that she doubted him. Had he become, in her eyes, a rival for the Lowry money? Good God.

"When was the last time you saw Mother?" Sharon asked.

Roger Dowling wished he had not come to lunch. He wished he had suffered Sylvia's calls in silence. He felt he was being drawn into a web of avarice and greed.

"Not much more than an hour ago," he said.

3

SYLVIA LOWRY knew they must think her crazy; there were times when she thought so herself. Had she really telephoned Father Dowling in the middle of the night? What must the man think of her? At Mass she had knelt in her accustomed place, trying to appear both nonchalant and devout. You would think it should be easy to pray, but she found it almost impossible. Daily Mass seemed no more spiritual an exercise than a daily walk might be. Of course she drove to St. Hilary's. It was important to stay active and independent, to get about by herself, to take care of herself. If she had to rely on others, let those others be strangers. Like the television repairman, she thought with sudden brightness. She liked him, and he seemed to enjoy talking to her. He told her about his other customers, gossip, anecdotes; it was shameless to listen and even to prod him on. He would also give her unintelligible explanations as to why she was having trouble with her set. Last week the trouble was that the set was unplugged. Sylvia had thought he was joking, but sure enough, the plug lay on the floor behind the set. How on earth had that happened? He would not charge her for the call so she had offered him coffee and doughnuts. At the kitchen table they discussed the mystery of the unplugged TV. The best solution seemed to be that it had been jostled loose by the vacuum.

"Better tell your maid to be more careful," he said, peering at her over the hand with which he wiped his mouth.

"My maid! I have no maid."

"Well, whoever does your house cleaning."

"I do my own house cleaning. I always have."

This was true, but he seemed skeptical. Did she seem rich to him? No doubt. It was difficult to know just what it means to be rich. No, that wasn't so. It meant that one's children wanted one dead. They wished she would die. At midday, distracted at Father Dowling's Mass, this seemed a thought like any other. But she was not a burden, not a nuisance, that wasn't it. They wanted her money.

Well, they were not going to get it. She had made up her mind to that years ago. It was money that had spoiled them in the first place, as she had warned August it would. But he had been so eager to lavish on them what he had never had—private schools, automobiles, the country club. No wonder the children had grown up as they had. How many Catholics had they known during their formative years? Their ideals, their vision of life, were materialistic. Small wonder they had turned out as they had.

And they had broken August's heart. Sharon got married on some army base in California when she knew her father had dreamed of a huge wedding for her. St. Hilary's gleaming as it never had before, a reception at the club, everyone there, a honeymoon trip. And in the end there had been nothing but a telegram informing them that Sharon and Bill Cordwill had been married in the base chapel one October day in 1952. She had warned August about a girl traveling halfway across the country in wartime. Is this trip necessary? Thank God it had not been necessary in the way Sylvia had feared. That would have been the death of August.

Sylvia looked about her. St. Hilary's had survived the changes in the neighborhood. It was still a beautiful church. Even on a day as hot as this it really was not necessary to have the fans going. This was the church in which she and August had been married so long ago, by Father Cleary with his lantern jaw, ill-fitting teeth, and rimless glasses resting on his bulbous nose. She could still see his clear blue eyes when he instructed them on the seriousness of marriage. Think of it. All these years later she could still walk into the church she had entered as a bride. What would have happened to that Quonset hut of a chapel Sharon and Bill had been married in? How she had cried over the snapshots. Did that chapel exist anywhere now except in those snapshots? She imagined that it had long since been torn down. Better to think that than to imagine it rotting away in California, waiting for another war.

It was Bill Cordwill who had made inquiries at the bank and found out that she was not following Henry Bradshaw's advice. Of course Henry had told him. So much for professional confidence. Imagine what August would have done if his banker or lawyer had discussed his affairs with a third party, even a relative. Such communications had been sacred, binding in secrecy, almost like the seal of the confessional. The worst thing about being old was that you lost the privileges of an adult. Would Father Dowling talk to her family too? Well, why on earth wouldn't he, being wakened in the middle of the night? It was not as if she had confided to him in the confessional.

When she went to confession now she found herself dredging up sins of years before. She had a dread of appearing before the throne of God with unforgiven sins upon her soul. Sometimes she had a horrible dream in which she had committed a mortal sin and then forgotten it, lived out her life in the delusion that she was in the state of grace, and then, at death, discovered the horrible truth. Father Dowling had been patient but scarcely reassuring.

"When I give you absolution it is for all your sins."

"Even those I haven't confessed?"

"Yes."

"But don't I have to mention mortal sins?"

"Is there something you haven't told me?"

"I don't know. I may have forgotten."

"Are you sorry for the sins you do remember, and for all the sins of your past life?"

"Yes!"

That was so easy to say, but she meant it, she really did. She certainly wanted to mean it. How useless her life seemed when she looked back upon it now. Was it contrition she felt or only a sense of having lived in vain? She should be able to take pride in her children, but she could not. Perhaps it was her failure with her children that she wanted to confess.

"I am sure you were a good mother," Father Dowling said. He could not keep the long-suffering from his voice, the poor man, but at least he tried. "Now, for your penance, say five Our Fathers and five Hail Marys and make a good act of contrition."

What she had to avoid above all was loading her sense of failure with the children onto August. She did not want to accuse him now. She was quite willing to take all the blame, since she still had the chance to make amends, whereas August . . . She stopped the thought. She did not want to think of where he—or, to be more accurate, his soul—was now. Purgatory, pain, waiting for what must seem an eternity but was not—Oh, she must pray for him more than she did.

She bowed her head, shutting out the sound of the fans, shutting out the sound of Father Dowling busy at the altar. Her lips moved silently. She might have been speaking to August rather than to God. She told him she would use the money for prayers, she would make certain that many many Masses would be said to free him from the fires of purgatory.

THE OFFICES of Anthony Mendax Enterprises, Inc., were located in a converted house in what had once been a posh residential area in Kenosha. A brick house, painted white, charcoal shutters, the merest wisps of new ivy on the walls, and along the front walk and bordering the drive a new box hedge scarcely more than two feet high. It was a narrow house with high surprised windows. In the back yard were huge oaks in, around, and off which lived several dozen squirrels, tame beasts who hopped down the walk to greet the mailman and infrequent visitors. A tasteful sign stood at the conjunction of driveway and walk, the legend Anthony Mendax Enterprises, Inc. lettered in black on an olive green background. There was no indication of the nature of said enterprises.

They were legion, taken all in all, in series if not at the present time. The front door opened on an erstwhile hallway, bare but for a mirror on the right-hand wall and a small table beneath the mirror. The visitor's eye was led up the stairway immediately before him to a landing where huge windows cast whatever light they caught through the oaks onto the pale green carpet that covered the hallway and ran up the stairs. To the right a receptionist. The décor, the appointments, suggested the office of an architect, an interior decorator, perhaps a commercial artist. There was the tang of creativity in the air.

The receptionist, fiftyish, a beneficiary of Weight Watchers, had been with Mendax from the beginning and was likely to remain with him to the end. Indeed, on several occasions she had thought she had. Now, like a gambler too far down to quit, like one whose initial innocence could not possibly have survived the years with Mendax and who thus might be regarded as an accomplice after the fact, or perhaps only like one whose curiosity as to when the juggling would cease and Mendax stand defeated on the stage, the balls, the spinning plates, the Indian clubs clattering all about him in a seemingly inevitable, dreaded, but secretly wished-for finale, she kept to her desk against her better judgment.

To the left of the hallway, glass doors. Closed. Behind them, Anthony Mendax. He is in his mid-forties and looks ten years younger. His skin has the dry look of an alcoholic's, his hair is still black, the trace of gray theatrical, too perfect, contributing to a vague untrustworthiness. A nervous man, compulsive, a chain smoker, dressed in a style meant for the young but that might nonetheless have been designed just for him. A suit of denim, white stitching, oversized lapels, tieless shirt, suede ankle-high shoes of curious design. Mendax is studying the layout of a new brochure as he paces the office. Educational film clips, a new ruse, his hope to drain money from the school boards of the Midwest. The brochure suggests without overtly saying it that the film clips were created, produced, filmed, and processed by Anthony Mendax Associates. But the half-hour film strip of the Lewis and Clark expedition, that on the Conquistadores, that on the California Missions, that on the Jesuit Martyrs of North America, that on Little Big Horn, the dozen each devoted to the Revolutionary and Civil Wars respectively—all were picked up for a song from a bankrupt entrepreneur in Oshkosh who had gone broke trying unsuccessfully to do what Mendax was sure he himself could do, even at a time when the slice of the tax dollar going to education was diminishing and conglomerate empires in New York were cornering the audio-visual racket and squeezing out the little guy. These films and accompanying tapes and records, the rental projectors, represented the current capital investment of Anthony Mendax Enterprises, Inc., not to mention that of Anthony Mendax Associates. They were underwritten by the last bank loan short of success Anthony Mendax could hope to negotiate in Kenosha. That he was involved in what could well be his last chance only added zest to his days, a zest, however, that had had to overcome recurrent doubt during the month since he had bid successfully for the inventory of the Oshkosh firm.

The glass doors opened and the receptionist entered with the mail. She dropped it on the huge mahogany desk that stood equidistant between two windows whose dark green drapes were pulled against the curious. At the far end of the room was a large fireplace; its marble mantel gave a baronial touch to the office.

"What do you think of this, Marge?"

She took the crinkly sheet and held it at arm's length, a frown on her face. Any sensation of *déjà vu,* of having been down this path before, remained her secret. She nodded her head sagely.

"Nice."

"Nice!" Mendax dealt in superlatives, an inflated coin. *"Very* nice. How will you pay the printer?"

He smiled. O ye of little faith. "That is the artist's problem. We deal only with him."

"I can write maybe ten more checks and that's it."

"Why ten?"

"I'm thinking of salary."

"Aha."

"There's the mail."

He nodded. He was in the never-never land of this new scheme. That this was July and long past time for the visual aid departments of school boards to have allocated their funds did not bother him. He had reason to trust his powers of persuasion. An unpersuasive Mendax would long since have been in jail, or in despair.

The glass doors closed. He sat at his desk, laying the artwork before him. His eye was caught by the pile of mail but darted away. Mail meant bills, threats, bad news. Good news came viva voce or by phone. He inhaled bravely, picked up the mail, and began to deal it out upon the desk. All discards but one, a small pale blue envelope addressed in a wavering hand to Anima Mundi Books. Good Lord, how long ago had that been? He tipped back in his chair, tapped his chin with the envelope, remembered.

At least fifteen years ago. This same house, although

it had not yet been redecorated. He had tried to get in on the bonanza he was sure lurked in the racks that stood in the vestibules of churches—pamphlets, devotional literature, tracts, at a dime a throw. Sell them in bulk to ministers and priests, develop a clientele. Once initial costs were met, the rest would be gravy. His enthusiasm returned as he remembered, no matter that he had lost his shirt on the deal. Even now the attic of this house was filled with grim piles of brown paper packages containing thousands of unsold pamphlets. With a wistful smile on his lips, Mendax opened the letter.

Anima Mundi Books
141 Damascus
Kenosha, Wisconsin

Dear Fathers,

I am a widow of seventy-five whose thoughts turn ever more to the next world. Your pamphlet, *The Rosary and the End of the World,* I have read many times. It frightens me but I am sure that it has done me much good. I wish to give you some money to help you in your work. A sum of fifty thousand dollars. In return I shall want the soul of my husband to be remembered in your prayers, especially in your Masses. Please let me hear from you. If one of your priests cannot come to Fox River I will come up to Kenosha.

Sincerely,
(Mrs.) Sylvia Lowry
603 Bering Street
Fox River, Illinois

Anthony Mendax read it again, slowly. Fathers? The poor dear was confused. The handwriting seemed authentically that of an old woman. The postmark looked authentic enough, though he did not claim to understand the crazy new system. But he could check to see if it had really been mailed in Fox River. He depressed a button on the intercom.

"Marge?"

"Uh, huh."

"Marge, do you know those packages upstairs, the ones with our pamphlets in them?"

"Are they still around?"

"They better be. Go up and see if you can find me a copy of . . ." He picked up the letter to check the title. "A copy of *The Rosary and the End of the World.*"

5

JIMMY LOWRY was between wives. And not in the way you're thinking, he would add with a polygamist leer. He was not a large man, 5′10″, but his torso was short and his legs were long and he gave the impression of height. The dirty talk seemed a mask behind which his cunning could proceed undetected and unfeared. The conventional wisdom is that he who talks is not doing. Perhaps. But there was a look of corrupt youth about Jimmy. What little hair he had left grew on the sides of his head, but by ingenious teasing, puffing, rerouting and spraying, Jimmy's barber more or less concealed the skin of

Jimmy's skull. Gray mutton chops, the fine Lowry nose and gray-green eyes, the corners of Jimmy's crinkled in perpetual bonhomie as Sharon's were from squinting into the sun.

James Lowry, D.D.S.–it was difficult to think of him as a dentist, with a drill in his hand, pawing around in people's mouths. Jimmy had practiced until his father's death, and then had turned his full attention to the management of his labs, clinics, and office buildings. It was one of Bill Cordwill's lesser ambitions to find out what Jimmy was really worth.

"Martha has been painting in Europe," Jimmy informed them. Martha was on the trustworthy side of thirty, an ample woman who had a way of leaning over the table, to follow what Jimmy was saying or to look sincerely at the Cordwills. Bill, distracted by the lovely melonlike breasts her inclination revealed, forgot his annoyance that Jimmy had brought her uninvited.

"It was something I had always wanted to do," she confided. She might have been reciting her creed. Discover what you really want to do and then do it.

"I once studied abroad myself," Jimmy chirped. "Then I married her."

Only Martha, for whom Jimmy's jokes were new, laughed.

"Do you paint in oils?" Sharon asked dutifully.

"Water color."

"What is the color of water?"

"Oh Jimmy."

Sharon and Bill exchanged a look. The idea of this dinner was to talk to Jimmy about Sylvia Lowry. Why the hell had he brought Martha? Apparently she had moved in with him. It was clear that she had been ripe for him. Convinced that the half dozen years of her crumbled marriage had thwarted and confined her, she was now in pursuit of her real self. Sharon's suggestion that they have coffee in the living room had the quaint force of hinting to Martha that they leave the gentlemen to their port.

"Does she really paint, Jimmy?" Bill asked when they were alone.

"She'd better."

Bill got out of range of Jimmy's nudging elbow. "We've got to talk about your mother, Jimmy."

"What about Mother?" Jimmy dropped his sophomoric manner and studied Bill with those gray-green eyes. Bill felt in the presence of the man behind the mask.

"You know about your mother, Jimmy. She is going around telling people we want her dead."

"We?"

"She called up a priest at three in the morning to tell him she is scared to death."

"Who isn't at three in the morning?"

"She can't go on doing this."

"Maybe she's right, Bill. Do *you* want her to live on and on into driveling senility?"

"Sharon and I think you should talk to her."

"And say what? Please don't tell people your family wants you dead? Please don't call up the priest in the middle of the night? What priest?"

"Father Dowling. The new pastor at Saint Hilary's."

"Saint Hilary's," Jimmy mused. It would have been some time since Jimmy had been inside a church. "Saint Hilarious. And the good Father came to you?"

"To Sharon."

"Does he think Mother is off her nut?"

"I don't know."

"But you think so, don't you, Bill?"

"What would anyone think, Jimmy? Tell me that."

And Bill explained about the bank, the withdrawals. It was difficult to keep the puzzled anger out of his voice.

"Okay, okay." Jimmy showed the palm of his hand. "'What is Dowling like?"

"I don't know what Dowling's like," Bill said impatiently. "Will you talk to her?"

"Yes, I'll talk to her."

"When?"

"Tonight."

"Good! This has really upset Sharon, Jimmy."

"Thrown her game off, has it?"

In the living room the women were talking of children. Apparently Martha had a son. "He's a nice boy, isn't he, Jimmy?"

"All boys are nice."

"You weren't," Sharon said.

The laughter was joyless. Jimmy did not like the topic of children. No wonder. He is a cold bastard, Bill Cordwill thought. For that matter, so was Sharon. She sat on the couch, cool, serene, as if she had spent the day on the golf course. August Lowry had been the only one of them Bill Cordwill understood.

When Jimmy and Martha were gone, Bill told Sharon of her brother's promise.

"Is he taking Martha with him?"

"He didn't say. I hope so."

"Could you imagine mother's reaction to that woman?" Sharon shuddered and looked away.

They were upstairs when the phone rang an hour later. Bill answered it. Sharon looked out of the bathroom, toothbrush in her mouth.

"Are you serious?" Bill said into the phone.

"Scout's honor," Jimmy said.

"Your mother isn't home."

"I just told you that," Jimmy said.

"I'm telling Sharon. Jimmy, is the car there?"

"Nope. And she left the garage door open."

"Well, I'll be damned."

"No doubt. Bill, she is probably out playing bingo or making a novena."

"She shouldn't be driving at all, let alone at night."

"Well, I wanted you to know I tried."

"I'll take it from here, Jimmy."

"Take it where, for Christ's sake?"

"Has it occurred to you that she might have left home?"

"Do you want us to wait here until she gets back?"

"No. I said I'd take care of it. You and Martha just go."

"Well, thanks a helluva lot, Bill. I think we will."

Bill called Father Dowling first. The pastor of St. Hilary's had no idea where Sylvia Lowry was and he was surprised, if Bill Cordwill was any judge, that he should be asked.

"I think I should call the police."

"You're really that concerned?"

"Yes, Father. I am."

When Father Dowling mentioned Phil Keegan, it seemed a triumph for ESP, although Bill had not known Dowling was acquainted with the chief of detectives. Calling Keegan was ideal. It sufficiently expressed their concern without making it a fully official matter.

6

DURING the years he had labored on the Archdiocesan Marriage Court, Roger Dowling had feared that the phrase "until death do us part" might prove a better description of his tenure on the court than it did of the unions of those couples who, reduced to the status of cases, paraded past the skeptical canonical eye in quest of an annulment.

In the beginning he had been excited by his work, more hopeful that a truly novel explanation lay behind estrangement of spouse from spouse. Eventually the repetition, the law's delay, the not-quite-honesty on all sides and the relative helplessness of the tribunal, outpost as it was of a bureacracy thousands of miles away where the truly difficult, truly interesting cases must be sent for decision—eventually all these took their toll.

Fortunately, his *modus operandi* had been developed during the first naïve years of his assignment when it had seemed that with care, with precision, with thoroughness, the knottiest problem could be resolved: the law served, the petitioners freed of their burden and released to a better future. But even what should have been routine cases, clear instances of forced consent, for example, continued to consume time even after the most painstaking gathering of depositions and evidence. Couples seemed to age before his eyes while hope died in theirs. Long before any ecclesiastical disposition, they would obtain a civil divorce, thus complicating their dossier, excommunicating themselves, and creating another heap of canonical problems for some future heads to worry over. In chancery. Once he had thought Bleak House a typical Dickensian exaggeration. There were days when it seemed the soberest report of the actualities of the legal, both civil and ecclesiastical.

He had served on the court for more than fifteen years. It had been his principal, indeed his only work. Attendance at conventions of canon lawyers ceased to attract after the first years. There was little relief to be had from learning that one's own woes were multiplied a hundredfold across the land. He read *The Jurist,* wrote several pieces for it, became a regular reviewer for it and other journals of canon law; he worked very hard. He became an acknowledged expert in the institution from which he had excluded himself by his promise of celibacy; like St. Paul before him, he saw it as a great mystery and, like a medical man, he guessed at the existence of a healthy specimen by negating the samples he encountered. And began to hate his work. Hated it yet felt wedded to it by more than the will and appointment of the Cardinal Archbishop of Chicago. Each new case seemed an extension of his sentence, and there would always be new cases, a steady endless flow like that of time itself. And each case represented people, at least two persons, as often as not children too, and, in the shadows, a third adult, an all-too-interested party seldom explicitly alluded to. To initiate a process was to wish to be freed from a marriage. At least one of the parties already knew how she or he would use that freedom regained, how lose it again, perhaps as heedlessly as before.

It was difficult not to feel somehow outside and above the stream of humanity, an increasingly knowledgeable observer. Dear God, the foibles, the weaknesses of the human heart. If nothing else, he had become an acute student of the species. Yet the final scab would not form on his heart, he could not become a mere functionary and bureaucrat. He continued to see, beyond the documents and dossiers, faces, destinies, souls. Tragedy and comedy. Impotence, its victims hostile to the celibate court; allegations of nonconsummation, with two or three children as proof that the age of miracles is not past. Most cases were foredoomed, no annulment possible, the marriage as valid as could be. It was these that presented the greatest potential for trouble: false testimony, perjury, the mad hope that sprang up in people that they could use the Church against herself, pay deference to the notion of the indissolubility of a validly contracted marriage while wringing from the archdiocesan court the judgment that their own union was not valid in the canonical sense. One had to listen with sympathy, be both benevolent and skeptical, be judge, advocate, and prosecutor in turn. It was essential that hope be not stirred where none was warranted and equally that an unfounded despair be avoided.

Souls. He felt like Dante being led through hell and purgatory. Nor was the simile casual. He became a Dante scholar of sorts and God only knew to what degree he owed his survival, partial survival, of those fifteen years to the vision of the great Florentine. It became possible to see that his cases, the people he met, were not exceptions, statistical anomolies in the Church and in the wider society. That had been his notion at the start, of course. These poor couples had wandered from normalcy and the task was to return them to the mainstream. The mainstream. But elsewhere were only different kinds of failure and weakness, different problems. The world was, in the phrase, a vale of tears. A mordant realization, perhaps, but it had made it possible for him to go on.

His hair thinned, revealing the narrow domed skull that was the repository of so much borrowed human grief. Like many tall people, he had early acquired a slight stoop and, as he grew older, sadder if not wiser, his posture suggested that he was willing to shoulder whatever tragedy was brought to him. In a rare moment of vanity, it had occurred to him that his face was not unlike Dante's, but the resemblance, as another would have noticed, stopped with the eyes. The great Florentine had relished the role of judge, consigning with equanimity his foes to choice states of torture. Roger Dowling's eyes smoldered with mercy and he took on a lidded look to conceal at least partially his vulnerability to others' pain. When, in consultation or at a hearing, he drew his long-fingered hands down his cheeks, his face became a tragic mask, but the pity in his eyes might have been the world's last hope. He found it necessary to cultivate a dignified reserve. Impeccably dressed in clericals, his Roman collar seemingly a centimeter higher and a shade whiter than anyone else's, he never came to be regarded as a full-fledged ecclesiastical functionary.

He was known to be deeply affected by his cases. Not that his problems were theological. Aquinas and Dante saved him from presumptive intellectual pride. It was the mystery of the relation between justice and mercy that haunted him. He was content to leave it a mystery. Indeed, he was convinced it must be a mystery. How could a merciful God permit whole lives to be wasted, caught by what seemed a mere legal technicality? Increasingly after Vatican II, he heard canonists echo the intellectual bankruptcy of the moral theologians. He predicted before it came the floodtide of annulments, the product of cynicism parading as mercy. Is there a human self distinct from the history of its deeds, a self that can be freed from what it has done, from what it is, and still be, still exist? In such enigmatic rhetorical questions was his own conviction distilled. He no longer saw the people who came before the court as different. It was when the marriage court no longer seemed to deal in anomaly but only with life writ small that he began to drink.

He had always drunk in the harmless sense, a sherry before lunch perhaps, a martini or two in the evening, infrequently more than two at a clerical bash. He began to drink as if he were fulfilling a destiny awaiting him all along. He drank alone, he drank in the morning after saying Mass but before beginning the work of the day, he welcomed the mask of the ordinary rituals permitting drinks at meals, the innocent public consumption. He drank at night. Was he ever sober, completely sober? Was he ever completely drunk? He was a lush in limbo, able to do his work; he never failed to be at his office; so far as he knew he had not given scandal, not for a long time, not for a year. But it was as if he had died within. Offering Mass, reading his breviary, trying to meditate, all became mechanical. He tried to stop drinking and he succeeded, many times, going a day, even several days, once almost a month, without a drink. His head would become light, his skin hypersensitive, the world seemed to assault him in its uncushioned thereness. Once in court he could not stifle a sob. He lapsed.

His weakness helped his work. The vantage point of the observer could no longer satisfy. He felt at one with other humans whose weakness had brought them low. His thoroughness and efficiency did not noticeably suffer. In an odd way, despite the dryness he felt saying his Mass and office, he felt closer to God. He had a greater claim on the divine mercy now. He could not regard himself as a clerical success, one of the elite who had been sent off for a doctorate and brought back to help tend the machinery of the largest archdiocese in the world. He was a member of the group from which future bishops are taken. No doubt he had taken pride in that. His drinking humbled him; he saw his ineradicable need for forgiveness. He recognized the mystery of justice and mercy: Mercy is what we pray for; justice is what we dread.

He began to daydream of his future. The only reward he wanted as repayment for a life spent in the clerical bureaucracy was a country parish in which he could live out the remainder of his priestly days, ministering to a simple flock, beloved perhaps, pottering about his rectory, studying, reading, praying. Tears filled his eyes when he thought of the spiritual life he might develop if freed from the Archdiocesan Marriage Court. How did he differ from the benighted petitioners longing to escape a bad marriage? The future he dreamed of was part Trollope—a Victorian vicar with an assured living in a rural setting—but it had its priestly, even monkish, side. It was as if God could no longer be found in the city but had withdrawn to the countryside.

The first time drink brought on a blank period, a day for which he could not account, nothing resulted. He had not gone to his office, he had not answered his phone when his secretary called his rooms, but all assumed that some urgent business explained his absence. To be physically away was one thing, but to have vacated his mind was a frightening thing—absence indeed. He did not drink for a week. Was he even surprised when it became clear to him that others knew he drank? He realized, it was as if he had always known it, that he was looked upon with the slightest condescension though not quite askance. Only his brilliance, his thoroughness, his knowledgeability concerning so many active cases, saved him. But inevitably the time came when he passed some alcoholic milestone and he knew that reprieve was near.

"It is a form of suicide," the doctor said.

His name was Sangretti. Dowling sat in his sun-filled office in the sanitarium in Wisconsin. Bars of sunlight slanted through the room, roiled with cigarette smoke. Sangretti snuffed out his cigarette and lit another.

"Like smoking?" Dowling asked.

The doctor contemplated the ash of his cigarette as if it were a bust of Homer. He nodded, conceding the point.

"Like smoking. Tell me about your work."

"I am a lawyer. A canon lawyer."

"I see."

But it was clear that Sangretti did not see. Dowling gave him the briefest of sketches of the life he led.

"And you hate it."

Hate it? He had never said aloud that he hated his work. What were those lines of Auden? *An unimportant clerk writes I do not like my work on a pink official form*?

"It is difficult, certainly. I don't mean physically onerous. It is sad work."

"The people you deal with are sad?"

"Yes."

Sangretti hunched forward. They were colleagues in a way.

"Unhappy? Unable to deal with their conflicts?"

"They are so full of . . ." His eyes drifted from the doctor and went to the window. How green the world looked, how bright. "Of hope."

"Is that so bad?"

"They want a second chance. They are so sure they will do better if only they have a second chance."

"Perhaps they will."

"Perhaps."

"You don't believe it."

"Do you?"

Sangretti blew a stream of small smoke rings across his desk. "You cannot continue in your present work."

"That is not for me to say."

"You simply do what you are told?"

"I do what my archbishop tells me to do, yes."

The doctor rocked back in his chair, eyes narrowed. Dowling had become a specimen. But then Sangretti had become a specimen for Dowling. No, that was not true. A human being, someone not absorbed by the function he fulfilled in this office. Sangretti had spoken of conflicts. Did he have them himself? Physician, heal thyself. But that had been a taunt directed at Our Lord.

"If he told you to do another kind of work, would you do it?"

"Of course."

"Then ask for another assignment."

"I have been trained for the work I do."

"Surely there are others."

"I did not mean that I am indispensable."

"And a priest can do many things."

Dowling nodded. Many things, perhaps too many, but there is only one essential work of the priest. Mass, the sacraments, the care of souls. The marriage court could be seen as an extension of the last.

"I shall have to make a report, Father."

"And what will you say?"

"That for you to go on as you have been will kill you."

"I shall stop drinking."

"The drinking is only a symptom."

"Of what?"

"Of the fact that you hate your work."

"Hate is too strong a word."

"I do not think so. I do not think you think so."

There was a psychiatrist on the staff but Dowling refused to see him. He had the old-fashioned notion that such prying into the soul, guided only by a secular vision, was dangerous and wrong. It was a usurpation of the priest's role. What he wanted was forgiveness, absolution, mercy. He could not regard himself as a machine that had begun to malfunction.

He did quit drinking. It was surprisingly easy to do. And he went back to work on the marriage court, staying another half year.

"It won't be a city parish, of course," the chancellor said. He was a young man. The importance, if not the insolence, of office was strong upon him. He turned over some pages in the manila folder open upon his desk.

"It is very kind of the cardinal."

"You have had no parish experience, I see."

"Only some week-end work."

The chancellor grew thoughtful. "It needn't be a parish, Father. Look." He sat forward. "I'll be frank. About all you can get is someplace no one else wants. But there are other possible assignments, more appealing, less work, more in line with your experience."

"I have always wanted a parish."

"Chaplaincy of a school, a hospital chaplaincy. The school would be best. Mass, confessions, the rest of your time your own."

Dowling smiled and shook his head. He had an image of souls awaiting him, people actively engaged in life; he did not want to spend his days among the ailing or the young. Particularly not the young.

The chancellor got out a list of available parishes. They went to the wall and traced them on the map of greater Chicago. The manicured nail of the chancellor slid west from the city and came to a stop.

"There. Fox River. Not far from the expressway, you see. I suppose it is a bit of a bedroom place. Why don't you go take a look at it?"

"Who is there now?"

"It's vacant. The pastor died some months ago. The Franciscans have been looking after it; there was some talk of their taking it over, but that idea was dropped."

"That bad?"

"Oh, no. Manpower. They really don't have the men to staff it. I don't think they have been living in the rectory."

Dowling stepped closer to the map, as if its lines and colors would tell him more. Fox River was in a county south of McHenry and north of Kane.

"In and out for Mass, that was about it," the chancellor said. He meant the Franciscans.

"I'll go look at it."

"Good." The chancellor beamed like a realtor who had made a sale.

One look had been enough. Fox River was about forty miles west of the city, less than an hour's drive on Interstate 90. St. Hilary's was a downtown parish that had suffered while all else in Fox River had prospered from the westward movement of Chicago. It was this movement that explained the suburbs, satellite communities with their expensive uninspired housing spinning like subatomic particles around the asphalt nuclei of shopping centers. St. Hilary's was bisected, even trisected, by new roads; the parish had become divided from its self and its parishioners been siphoned off by the newer parishes, no matter the official diocesan boundaries. The church was Romanesque and huge, paid for and in good repair. The school had been discontinued. The rectory was presided over by Marie Murkin. She looked quizzically at the suitcase Dowling carried. He introduced himself.

"You're new."

"Yes."

"You going to stay here? Father Blaise never stayed."

She thought he was another Franciscan. Her pained expression told him how the fallen status of the parish affected her. She remembered, he was to learn, its golden days. He spent the day looking around. On the second floor he found the pastor's suite, a bedroom, a sitting room, a massive bath. A back porch looked out on the untended lawn. Through its screen windows the hum of the town and more distantly the whine of the interstate were audible. There were other rooms on the second floor, singles, three in all. On the first floor was a library-study, several parlors, the dining room and kitchen and Mrs. Murkin's quarters. At supper he told her he was the new pastor.

"Permanent?"

"Yes."

"You're the seventh."

"Since you've been here?"

The wrong thing to ask. She was not that old. "Of course I don't count the temporaries. Wait."

She brought him a typewritten manuscript bound in a loose-leaf notebook, the opus of Monsignor Hunniker, his immediate predecessor. The history of the parish. Dowling felt a mere appendage to this account of more stable and prosperous times. But he was attracted by the fading character of St. Hilary's. Its dim present, not its bright past, seemed an appropriate setting for the priest he had become.

For a time he really believed, as petitioners at the marriage court did, that life could be begun anew. He loved his parish, he loved the town, he loved the very dullness of the routine. Time spent in the confessional went swiftly, pious old women whispering their venial sins, the young caught up in the eternal battle with the flesh, children prattling in too-loud voices their lists of transgressions. How innocent they all seemed. He felt he had withdrawn from Carthage or Milan to Cassiciacum. Of course this could not last. It was silly at his age to think that sin is geographical, a feature of the city. The Trollope phase of his new life gave way quickly to the realization that the Fox River too ran through the valley of tears.

"You don't remember me," the man said, coming into the sacristy after the ten o'clock Mass one Sunday.

Dowling studied him. They were the same age and the face was vaguely familiar, but only in the way every face is vaguely familiar.

"Keegan."

Dowling repeated the name. Names on the tabs of manila folders slid past his mind's eye.

"Mundelein. I was at Mundelein."

"Ah."

"You were in the class ahead of me."

"You live in Fox River?"

Keegan nodded. "I left the seminary after a year of theology."

"Who could blame you?"

Keegan frowned but Dowling was relieved. He had wondered if Keegan might be a laicized priest and he had no idea what it would be like to have one in the parish. He asked Keegan what he did.

"I'm in the police department." He added gruffly, "Chief of detectives, not that that amounts to much in a town this size." But he was obviously proud of his status. "Where were you before Saint Hilary's?"

Others had come into the sacristy and were waiting to talk to the pastor. He suggested that Keegan stop by the rectory. They could have a long conversation there. He had only meant to be polite, but Keegan was delighted.

"How about tonight?"

"All right."

The Sunday-night visit became a ritual. Keegan was a widower and lonely and he liked to reminisce about the days when he had thought of becoming a priest. On his side, Dowling was curious about Keegan's work as a detective. So they traded tidbits of professional gossip and both were happy with the exchange. Keegan would come for supper and afterward they would talk in front of the television, play a little cribbage, watch the Cubs in night road-games or some other Chicago professional team disgrace itself before the most patient fans in the world. Keegan stayed until midnight.

Dowling enjoyed his visits. Who knows a town better than someone on its police force? Keegan revealed to him the hidden strata of this outwardly placid place. Keegan professed to be ever on the alert lest the mob got too close, but it seemed to Dowling that Fox River did pretty well on its own. What Dowling found surprising was Keegan's insatiable appetite for clerical gossip, even tales of the marriage court.

More than curiosity was involved in the avidity with which the seventh pastor of St. Hilary's listened to the detective. He was hearing of people, souls, human beings created for an eternal happiness. His prayers were for them; they were in his charge. If Keegan was the representative of justice, Dowling could feel that he represented mercy. It made them —old friends of a sort—antagonists.

This first became clear to Dowling when Sylvia Lowry's disappearance became a matter of police investigation.

7

THE TOASTER blew a fuse and Mrs. Murkin, normally a study in self-reliance, reported to him in panic.

"Do we have any new ones?"

"I wouldn't touch that fuse box, Father. The kitchen is overloaded anyway. A new fuse won't fix that."

Dowling calmed her. It was a way of soothing his own unease. The basement was the one part of the rectory he did not like. There were dank smells and corners unvisited by Marie Murkin's compulsive cleaning instinct. The floor inclined toward the drain and a wet stain there seemed the source of the odor. Dowling held the fuse before him like a talisman. He was all too aware of Marie in the doorway above. She had seen him off as if he were descending into a mine. The fuse box was beneath the stairs.

Dowling checked the floor beneath his feet. It seemed dry enough. There was an ominous sizzling sound from the metal box. Dowling hesitated. When he was a boy, nuns had used electricity as an example of a mystery we do not understand, a kind of steppingstone to belief in the supernatural. As a result he had never really tried to understand electricity. He remembered turning an emery wheel in the high school lab, but with the incredulity of a primitive.

"Be careful," Mrs. Murkin called.

"Don't worry."

Her remark seemed meant to discover if he was still alive. Pastor electrocuted in rectory basement. Shaking of heads and clucking of tongues in clerical gatherings for a week or so. Imagine Roger Dowling fooling around a fuse box. Perhaps an unspoken wonder. Had it really been an accident?

"Can you see, Father?"

The basement light had gone out with the one in the kitchen. Desmond the electrician had explained to him that all the kitchen lights and gadgets as well as the washer and dryer were bunched on the same circuit and that was bad. Dowling had his lighter out and he flicked it into flame. He assured Mrs. Murkin he could see.

"Let me call Desmond, Father. Let him fix it."

"I'll fix it."

Desmond would only stand here and shake his head and say again that the wiring in this house was a hazard and he would not be responsible. Desmond could say that while remaining oddly aloof. Technically he still lived in St. Hilary's parish but he and his family had defected to St. Teresa's. Dowling was getting used to the wariness of tradesmen where the Church was concerned. They dreaded being asked to make a contribution of their services. Why should they? The donor of a stained-glass window had his name put right into the glass, for all to see, though who now remembered the bearers of the names inserted in the beautiful windows in St. Hilary's church? Even Mrs. Murkin drew a blank on most of them. Desmond could not put a plaque on the fuse box commemorating his generosity.

Dowling found the blown fuse: its small window gone gray. Gingerly he unscrewed it. Did he only imagine that the hissing and crackling increased?

"How many air conditioners you got?" Desmond had asked.

"We have them in the bedrooms. And in the study," he added shamefacedly. Desmond made him feel he had overloaded the circuits for the sake of creature comfort.

In went the new fuse. Behind him the light went on and upstairs there was a cry of triumph from Mrs. Murkin.

"That's it, Father. You got it."

The light went out. So much for triumph. The new fuse too had blown. Dowling went upstairs to telephone Desmond.

After he had made the call and received Desmond's promise that he would send a man as soon as possible, Roger Dowling sat at his desk and felt out of his depth. The responsibility for the maintenance of the church and rectory weighed on him almost as much as the responsibility for the people of the parish. Failure with the parish plant would be more obvious than failure with souls.

Mrs. Lowry. Did he dare ask if she would consider picking up the tab for the rewiring Desmond would no doubt insist on now? Begging was something else he had not had much practice doing. He needed to discuss it with someone, someone other than Marie Murkin. Another man. He pulled the phone toward him and dialed Phil Keegan's number. But Keegan was not in his office. Dowling left a message. He hoped Phil would return his call before it was time to go say the noon Mass.

8

CAMELOT ESTATES consisted of apartments and town houses scattered ungeometrically along a swirl of roads, walls of distressed brick, mansard roofs, an artificial lake, the globes of the streetlamps an attractive hazard to kids with stones or slingshots. But of course there weren't any kids. Camelot Estates. Where these buildings stood Phil Keegan had hunted as a kid. Just north of where the artificial lake quacked with its dozen ducks had stood the copse of trees where they had found the body of the Fremont girl years ago. Rape. Murder. An unsolved case. All the unsolved cases. Keegan knew that the identified criminal class were but a fraction of the thieves and even murderers who walk the streets as innocently as you and I.

He hated his apartment. He spent as little time in it as he could. His wife had been dead ten years but he had kept the house until his daughters were grown and gone, married, both of them living hundreds of miles away in different directions. He had sold the house and taken this apartment and then had allowed himself to be conned into buying it when the new management transformed the place into condominiums. Able to remember when none of these buildings had been here, by lifelong habit an inhabitant of houses, Keegan felt in transit. But wasn't that life itself when you thought of it, being in transit?

He was a tall man, his body kept trim by savage games of handball in the gym. That cube of a court was the only place where he could be accused of police brutality. His hair was still thick, rising from his forehead as if in defiance of age. He kept it slicked down, but rain or a good sweat turned it into a silly mass of curls. That had always embarrassed him. He almost envied men who were bald. His lids veiled his eyes, giving him the look of a doubter, the look of one who has seen too much, a man for whom Diogenes with his lamp has too often turned out to be a Peeping Tom or arsonist. Anyone is capable of anything. And everyone must pay for what he has done. That was elementary. That was justice. Without justice, life would be a mockery.

Thank God for Roger Dowling. It was good to have him in town, good to have at least one evening of the week taken care of, one more evening. Keegan spent Mondays at the KC Hall—bowling, supper, a poker game afterward, the place usually crawling with people. Sometimes there was a dance, a testimonial dinner, a sports banquet for one of the schools, something. St. Vincent de Paul took care of Wednesdays. One night at Single Catholics had been enough. He had gone with the dread that he would be the oldest one there. Not by a long shot. Any faint notion he had had of marrying again was squelched by that one visit. An old doll whose smile seemed meant to display her dentures—did her dentist give her a discount as an advertisement?—had clung to him throughout the night, telling him of her son who was in the State Department, currently assigned to the consulate in Milan, she was so proud of him. As an afterthought, far too late, she had asked him about his own children. And he had denied having any.

Sometimes he actually doubted he did have two daughters, that he had once been married. Were his years as a cop a bad dream after all? He imagined he had stayed in the seminary, hung in there at Mundelein despite the fact that he had never been able to master Latin, and become a priest. It was difficult to recall why he had left. It must have been a fear of celibacy, the fear that he could not lead an unmarried life. He smiled sourly. Well, he had ended up a celibate, if not a eunuch, and for what? Not for the kingdom of heaven. Oh, he went to daily Mass, the noon Mass at St. Hilary's. Dowling could be trusted not to stage any liturgical extravaganzas. A straight simple Mass, done at a brisk but reverent pace. Keegan was out of the church by 12:30 with plenty of time for lunch before returning to headquarters.

Work was a blessing, a drug, the best distraction of all. He had wanted to tell Bill Cordwill that when he apologized for calling about his mother-in-law. Could anyone understand that he welcomed work, that he hated to leave his office at night, that on those nights of the week still unspoken for he worked overtime unpaid? Now that he was chief of detectives, no one noticed. The younger men probably thought he had to work around the clock.

On Tuesday, after Mass, he went into the sacristy and told Dowling about Sylvia Lowry.

"Then Cordwill called you?"

"How did you know?"

"Tell me about Mrs. Lowry."

"There's nothing to tell. She's gone. The family is worried. You can't blame them. The woman is well into her seventies."

"I know her."

"They had had a family powwow and the son Jimmy, he was a dentist." Keegan paused. "I guess he still is. Once a dentist, always a dentist. Like a priest." Keegan tried unsuccessfully to recall a Latin phrase. "Jimmy went to the house."

"And he discovered that she had gone?"

Keegan nodded. "They're worried about the way she's been acting lately."

"You mean her fear of dying?"

Keegan shook his head. "The way she's been handling money."

"I see."

"I haven't got the details. Anyway, they were concerned. Jimmy went to talk to her, as delegate of the family, but she had vamoosed."

"I noticed that she wasn't at Mass today."

"She attends the noon Mass?"

"I thought you knew her."

"No."

"She's always in the same pew, up front, on the left."

"Wears a hat?"

"Yes. Yes, she does. I hadn't noticed. I gather you haven't found where she went."

It was not a story Keegan wished to hurry through. "After Cordwill called me, I went over there."

"Last night?"

"He called me at home this morning. At seven. I went to the house from my apartment."

"And?" They had left the sacristy and were standing on the walk leading to the rectory. The midday heat descended like a malevolent hand upon them. Keegan seemed not to notice.

"Nothing. The house was empty."

"You went inside?"

"The door was unlocked."

"Isn't that odd?"

"I was told it would be."

"Jimmy Lowry left the house unlocked?"

"Look, Roger, a locked door is no protection at all."

"Don't ever tell Sylvia Lowry that. She is a bundle of fears."

"Her bed hadn't been slept in. That didn't surprise me, of course. I had been told her car was gone, and it was. The garage empty, the door open. She must have left on the spur of the moment."

"Why do you say that?"

"There was luggage in the attic and there was a suitcase in her closet."

"She might have used another."

"And the television had been left on."

Dowling thought about that, lighting his pipe as he did so. "Jimmy Lowry?" he suggested.

But Keegan shook his head.

"I don't mean that it was on this morning. Jimmy turned it off last night."

"Then Mr. Cordwill told you she had left it on."

"That's right."

"Look, why don't you have lunch with me? We'll get a sunstroke standing here."

"If you're sure it's no trouble." But Keegan had already started toward the house.

"Mr. Keegan likes beer with his meal," Dowling told Marie when they were ensconced at the table.

"If it's no trouble," Keegan said.

Mrs. Murkin brought the beer in a bottle and plunked it down at Keegan's elbow, together with an opener.

"Ah, the church key."

"What next? About Sylvia Lowry?" Dowling had

waited until Marie returned to the kitchen and the murmur of her television.

"The family filed a missing person report. The fact that she took the car is a big help. It is a lot easier to trace a car than a human being."

"God knows we all have enough numbers attached to us."

"But not to our rear ends."

"She was frightened of her family, Phil. She actually said she thought they wanted her dead."

"How do you know that?"

"It was not a confidence. The night before last she called me at three in the morning. I managed to calm her down."

"Did you tell anyone else?"

"I went to Sharon Cordwill."

"Hmm."

"Of course it was a delusion."

"Why did she think they wanted her dead?"

"Money."

"Money?"

"Surely she has some, doesn't she?"

"It doesn't make sense. Jimmy Lowry is rolling in money and Bill Cordwill is a prosperous man. Any money she has would not be that big an attraction to them."

"I think she's disappointed in her children."

"The Church?"

He nodded.

"They certainly aren't pillars, are they?"

"They're not in my parish, of course."

Keegan sensed that Dowling was drawing a veil over the subject and he respected him for it. The best thing about their friendship was that they could both unwind, speak freely, and not worry that curiosity would lead the other to presume on their friendship and go too far.

"I never thought of Sylvia Lowry as a TV addict."

"All old women are TV addicts." Keegan dipped his head in the direction of the kitchen.

"You may be right."

"She might have kept it on for company."

That made sense; still it was an odd thought, an old woman alone in her house, the roar of the television her reassuring link with the outside world. And then she leaves the house and the television continues to blather on in the empty rooms. Roger Dowling found it highly implausible for Sylvia Lowry to have gone off like that.

"Did you search the house, Phil?"

"From top to bottom."

"You did mention the attic."

"And I went down into the basement. I searched every closet. Don't worry."

"Don't worry?"

"I mean, don't think that she had a stroke or something and is lying helpless in that house. She went away, all right. There's no doubt about it."

"Speaking of basements," Dowling said, "what do you know about fuses?"

9

IF IT WERE not for Edna Hospers, Father Dowling thought, the parish might sink even deeper into somnolence. The thought was almost wistful. Edna was, in the categories she loved to employ, a Young Mother, and we all know that Young Mothers can go squirrely, cooped up with their kids for days on end, their conversation never above the level of Captain Kangaroo, so Edna had this idea, and she knew Father Dowling would agree as soon as he heard it—could he have dared to disagree after such fanfare?—and anyway didn't the parish have an obligation to do things like this for the parishioners? They contributed, didn't they, and some of them, like Edna and her husband, Gene, had lived in St. Hilary's all their lives. Her idea was this: once a week, during the afternoon or maybe the morning would be better, there would be a get-together in the parish hall, women with their kids, coffee, cards, a little adult conversation for a change.

"Well, if enough people are interested . . ."

"Thank you, Father. I'll get a committee together, some people who have Always Been Active."

In the event, the idea had spread beyond Young Marrieds to Senior Citizens, widows, orphans, anyone at all, the halt and the lame, the unemployed—Edna and her committee gathered them in from highway and byway, gave them a wedding garment, bade them welcome. There were classes in ceramics, in drawing, there were lessons in cooking and crewel. Dowling himself was induced to give a lecture on new trends in Catholic thought. The topic was assigned him. He used it as an opportunity for satire. The New Testament is as new as anything need be.

"I've been wondering about a liturgy," Edna said one day. "Do you suppose . . ."

"No."

Edna, unused to opposition, was, for a change, wordless.

"I say Mass every day at noon, Edna. For the parish. Everyone is welcome."

"Yes, I know. But I thought . . ."

"No." He smiled. "You have done a wonderful thing with this weekly daytime get-together. Let's not spoil it."

"Well, you're the pastor."

"That's right."

Dowling had looked in the day they had Benson from the bank speak on savings, investments, stocks and bonds. To everyone's surprise, Sylvia Lowry had hounded the man with questions. Benson had been speaking with the ardor of an advocate of triple A bonds.

"They are so a risk," Sylvia piped.

Benson's brow got lost among his forelock. "Next to no risk at all, I believe I said."

"Companies default. They can and they do."

"Very well. Let us take Treasury certificates." He looked at Sylvia with an I-gotcha look. Did he know who she was? He had the wariness with which the public speaker probes his questioner to discover the nature of the adversary.

"You can have them," Sylvia said, and there was nervous giggling in the audience.

"Surely you won't call Treasury certificates a risk, Mrs. . . ."

But Sylvia did not give him her name. "Of course they are a risk."

"Then so is money itself," Benson said triumphantly. "They are as good as money."

"They can be discounted. You must pay to buy and sell them, unless of course you choose to drive into Chicago and wait in line at the Federal Reserve."

"You've made your point, Ma'am," Benson conceded, half turning from Sylvia. "There is some risk in Treasury certificates although they are, by common consent, in the present state of the market, the best and safest place to put your money. Money itself depreciates during inflation. There is always risk. I do not mean to mislead. But," and he turned to Sylvia with a wide false smile, "even breathing is a risk."

This inconclusive exchange had made Sylvia a minor heroine in the weekly group. Few of the others had had any inkling what Benson was talking about. Edna asked Sylvia if she herself would like to give a little talk.

"One we could understand," she said pointedly.

"Heavens no. What do I know about money?"

"You seemed to know a great deal."

"Mrs. Hospers, believe me, what I know about money could be put in a coffee can and buried in the yard."

"Let's have some coffee."

They sat at a card table near the wall, the three Hospers children on the floor about them. Sylvia was enthralled by the children.

"I know you won't believe a word of this," she said to Edna, "but these are the years you should cherish, your children young and innocent." Her voice drifted away and her eyes grew moist as she looked at little Rebecca Hospers, a lovely girl in smock and jeans and miniature tennis shoes who sat on the floor that she was pounding methodically with a long stick, the mortal remains of a hobby horse.

"How are your children?" Edna asked.

"Did you know them?"

"Only from a distance. Gene and I grew up in the parish, you know."

"What was your maiden name?"

"Monaghan."

Sylvia half closed her eyes in thought. "Monaghan."

"Plumbing and Heating."

"Why should she remember Monaghan Plumbing and Heating?" Gene asked, when she told him of the conversation. "We were the peasants, Eddie. People like the Lowrys don't even know the peasants exist."

"She's a sweet old lady."

"Look, I know the sweet old lady. I've worked on her set."

"I didn't know that."

"Big deal."

"What's it like?"

"Her television set?"

"No. The house."

Gene looked at her. He was a hulking giant of a man, yet still in appearance the boy she had known all her life. His denim shirtsleeves were rolled up over his elbows and his pants were too short, the way he liked them, exposing his white socks and black crepe-soled work shoes. He spoke as if he meant to punish her for asking. "A mansion. A goddam mansion. That little bird of a woman lives in a cage that would be big enough for two families."

Edna was sorry she had brought it up, not least because some of Gene's resentment crept into her own attitude toward Sylvia Lowry. It must be nice to be old and rolling in money and tell harried young mothers that these hectic years were the best years of their lives. Was that supposed to make her feel good and wise and caring? What became clear was that Sylvia was disappointed in her own children. She never said it in so many words, but she sighed and spoke of the crosses a mother must bear whenever the talk turned to what happened when kids became adolescents and then adults.

"I suppose it's heretical," Sylvia said, "but sometimes I think it is all a matter of blood, some long-ago forebear taking his revenge through a new member of the family."

Edna smiled and looked receptive. Heretical or not, it made the Lowry family less imposing to have Sylvia hinting at her disappointments.

"Of course it has to be heresy. If it were true, what difference would it make how we raise them, what we tell them? What difference would our prayers make?"

Sylvia's eyes went around the room full of bright predestined children at play. She smiled at Edna.

"Father Dowling would scold me if he heard me speaking like this."

The pastor did tend to treat Sylvia as if she were a child. From time to time he dropped in to see how things were going, giving his somewhat bewildered endorsement to all this activity. Several times he congratulated Edna on the success of her idea. As well he might have. He himself did not have to lift a finger and here was the liveliest thing that had happened to St. Hilary's for years humming along in the parish hall.

"Years ago there was the Saint Anne's Society," Sylvia remembered. "A very stuffy group. We got very dressed up and went to one another's homes. The children were always kept out of sight. This is so much more healthy."

"Incidentally," Father Dowling said, turning to Edna.

What a curious man he is, Edna thought.

"Marie's set is on the blink and she refuses to spend money to have it fixed. Would you have Gene come take care of it and send me the bill?"

"Gene Hospers!" Sylvia cried. "Why, I never made the connection. I know your husband. I am forever having trouble with my set."

"Are you blaming Gene?"

They all laughed, but Edna felt strangely deflated. The wife of the television repairman. How silly to be ashamed. But she was. It would have been hard not to be, given the way Gene resented the raw deal he considered his life to be. God only knew what Sylvia's husband had done.

"Everything," Gene said. "General contractor, that's how he got started. During the war he coined money. He ended up on the boards of the First Bank and half a dozen corporations."

"She seems to know all about money."

"Except how to spend it," Gene sneered.

10

"MR. KEEGAN called," Marie told him when he came back from the church where he had gone to read his breviary. It was amazing how cool the building remained, despite this heat. Besides, he liked to say his office in the presence of the Blessed Sacrament.

"Anything urgent?"

"He wants you to call him."

Marie Murkin's attitude toward Phil was ambivalent. At first she had been so expansive in her welcome that Dowling had wondered if she saw in Phil a possible replacement for the long-gone Murkin. She had brought them snacks, she had made certain Phil always had a fresh bottle of beer, she made the fateful suggestion of popcorn.

"Popcorn," Phil had said, turning to smile at Marie. "I love popcorn."

"Then I'll make some."

She did, and Phil wolfed it down like a kid.

"That really hit the spot," he said when he was done. He wiped his fingers carefully and picked up his cards.

"Would you like some more?"

"Better not."

Marie gathered up bowl and napkins and stood for a moment, but it was clear that Keegan had dismissed her from his mind. After that, she put the popcorn at Phil's elbow and disappeared.

"Was Mrs. Lowry at Mass today, Father?" Marie asked.

"No."

"Is it true she's missing?"

"Well, she's gone away without telling her family where."

"I don't blame her."

"Oh?"

Marie poured them each a glass of lemonade. "They're a bad crew," she said, handing Dowling his.

"In what way?"

"The son divorced, the daughter hanging around the country club. All she does is golf."

"It's good exercise."

"But what of her child?"

Dowling conceded the point and sipped his lemonade.

"There is a daughter named Cheryl. What kind of a name is that? Is there a Saint Cheryl?"

"Would you like me to look it up?"

"While you're at it, look up Sharon."

"How about Sylvia?"

"I wonder where she went."

"The car has been found," Keegan said. Busy office sounds came over the line to Dowling and he felt the slightest tug of nostalgia at the thought of that activity. "At O'Hare."

"So she could have gone anywhere?"

"If she left the car there."

"What do you mean?"

"Nothing. The fact that her car is found parked in a lot at O'Hare is not proof that she left it there."

"I suppose not."

"More likely than not, that is the explanation, of course."

"Then she could be anywhere."

"That's true in any case."

"Has the family any ideas?"

Keegan made an impatient noise. "Jimmy Lowry suggests we try Rome. He wanted to know if there isn't a Holy Year on or something."

"There is."

"I know."

"Has Sylvia been to Rome before?"

"Once. With her husband. In nineteen fifty."

"Another Holy Year."

"Which is what gave Jimmy the idea."

"I don't think so, Phil."

"Neither do I."

"Then where?"

"Was she at Mass today, Roger?"

"No."

"I couldn't make it. Because of the car."

"And the car doesn't tell you anything?"

"Not the preliminary check. She wasn't in the trunk, if that's what you're thinking."

"Good Lord. Why would I think a thing like that?"

"You think she hopped into her car, drove to O'Hare, and flew away?"

Dowling frowned at the drapes which hung at the study windows. Afternoon sun lay upon the folds of the fabric, eliciting soft tones from the dusty surface. He remembered the frightened voice of Sylvia on the phone. She did not seem the kind of person to be driven by delusion.

"No, Phil. I don't think so."

When he had hung up, he sat back in his chair. Before him an empty desk, an empty desk in an empty rectory, an uneventful afternoon before him. It had become his habit to take forty winks at various times throughout the day, a brief shallow sleep with the sounds of the town serenading him. Why not? He was out to pasture now, his active life behind him. This is what he had dreamed of.

His smile was sad. He had not dreamed of napping away his life. It had been his soul, not his body, he had hoped to tend to once he was free of the myriad distractions of the marriage tribunal. It was odd to think of that activity still going on, the laborious collection of information, the taking of depositions, the preparation of opinions. Meanwhile, the sad defeated couples waited, or did not wait, for the verdict, brooding on the putative injustice of the fact that one decision, one mistake, had misshaped their lives and deprived them of happiness. Happiness. The dream that would not die. But he himself had dreamed of happiness in this out-of-the-way rectory, free at last of canon law.

But he was a pastor, a shepherd of souls, his concern for Sylvia resided in that. No matter that she seemed an aging woman whose pampered life had not prepared her for her children's perfidy, her own fears. And were her fears unfounded? Improbable as it seemed, given the affluence of Sharon and Jimmy, it was money that explained Sylvia's unease. She was certain her children longed for her death. The only motive seemed money, and money seemed no motive.

"I'm not surprised," Bradshaw said, pushing back from his desk. He had seated himself after shaking Dowling's hand, pulled himself up to his desk and laid his hands flat upon it. Ready for business. The inquiry about Sylvia Lowry relaxed him. "She acted against my best advice."

"And what was that?"

"To leave her money in Treasury notes. In the present unsettled state of the economy, that is the safest, surest advice I can offer. Understand, it is not an *investment*. No, it is a species of *saving*."

Bradshaw's lips closed firmly on this dogma. "Now is a time to wait and see. Meanwhile, Treasury notes are paying ten percent, more or less, which is a very handsome return. I got her out of the market and into Treasury notes just in time."

"I see."

"Then, three months ago she sold them."

"In favor of what?"

Bradshaw's pale hands rose helplessly. "That's just it. She walked out of here with the *cash*."

"Quite a bit?"

Bradshaw seemed about to say how much and then stopped himself. "She did it in stages. She was almost cunning about it. First the money went into her safety deposit box and then, on half a dozen occasions, she paid visits to the bank. Would you like me to show you what I'm talking about?"

"All right."

They left Bradshaw's office on the second floor of the bank and crossed the large airy expanse of the investment department. They eschewed the elevator, going down a staircase of white and green marble, flanked on its open side by a brass handrail that gleamed from polishing. The noise of the business being conducted in the public area opening on the street rose to meet them. They crossed the marble floor, past lines of people waiting to transact their business at wickets. Dowling felt he had never been in a bank before, coming upon this scene from the quiet intensity of the area of Bradshaw's office. Marie Murkin did the parish banking, bringing the collection receipts down on Monday morning, going off in a taxi, the cash box nestled in the bottom of her shopping bag.

Bradshaw stopped at a counter. On the other side a wizened little man looked up curiously from his desk. Bradshaw indicated he was not required.

"In order to see one's safety deposit box, it is necessary to fill out one of these slips." He riffled the pages of a little pad. There were spaces to be filled in on the printed form: the number of the box, a signature.

"Rafferty checks the number and signature against a card in his file. Always. As far as bank policy is concerned, Rafferty has no memory for faces, he recognizes no one. If everything is in order, he escorts the renter to the vault."

They pushed through a swinging door that snapped shut behind them and walked toward the vault. Its huge door, opened, looked like a movable wall. Inside the vault, Bradshaw pointed out the boxes, which reminded Dowling of a post office.

"The customer has one key, Rafferty has another. Both are required to remove a box."

Dowling looked around. He felt he was learning more than he wanted or needed to know of the process. But Bradshaw was full of his subject.

"Then what?" Dowling asked.

"Out here."

They left the vault. Along the wall behind Rafferty was a row of doors. They looked like confessionals. Indeed, they were not much larger. Bradshaw opened a door to reveal a small built-in desk and chair. On the desk was what looked like an unreliable pen, a ball point with the name of the bank stamped on it, large envelopes, both white and khaki, a scratch pad. Dowling imagined a minor Midas fingering his possessions in the solitude of this little room. He imagined Sylvia Lowry seated there.

"She emptied the box in six trips," Bradshaw confided. "Bills of large denomination. Very large. They had to be in order to fit into the box that, as you have seen, is not large."

"But how do you know she emptied hers?"

Bradshaw hesitated. "Rafferty is absolutely reliable and discreet. The fact is, I told him to keep me informed of Mrs. Lowry's visits. I would be able to learn who had been in the vault in any case, of course. The slips."

"Then you suspected something?"

"Father Dowling, when a woman of seventy-five cashes in one hundred and fifty thousand dollars' worth of Treasury certificates and puts the money in a box, I worry. Do you realize what inflation does to that amount of cash in a matter of weeks?" There was a look of genuine pain on Bradshaw's face. "Any other course would have been preferable. A time deposit account. A checking account. At least some smidgin of interest to counteract inflation, if nothing else. Holding Treasury notes, she received a respectable annual return. As much as many people receive as salary." His eyes drifted to Rafferty, seated at his desk, on the job.

"She was seen to take money from the box?"

Bradshaw spoke carefully and in a whisper. "Rafferty knows that the last time he replaced the box it was empty."

"I suppose you spoke to Mrs. Lowry?"

"I tried to. It was hopeless." Bradshaw made an odd coughing sound, a laugh perhaps. "My guess is she had come to distrust banks. And bankers. Do you blame me for thinking she was losing her grip? No, I could not get through to her."

"And then?"

Bradshaw shut the door of the little room and drew Dowling back to the vault.

"Please understand, Father Dowling. Confidentiality is the essence of banking. In matters of money, the banker is his client's priest. It is a profound responsibility and one we do not take lightly. But sometimes, in special circumstances, it is just that responsibility which takes precedence over confidentiality. Do you follow me?"

"I think so." Bradshaw sounded like a canonist or, worse, a moral theologian. Perhaps his analogy of banker and priest was not as preposterous as Dowling wished to find it.

"Her family must have been alarmed."

"Of course they were alarmed. All that cash loose in the house. My God!"

"And they too failed to get through to her?"

Bradshaw nodded, abject. "Think of it, Father. Good Lord. That little old lady could be running around the country with a suitcase full of money."

"But why?"

"You tell me, Father. You tell me."

11

THE NEIGHBORHOOD did not look all that promising but the house was something else. Anthony Mendax drove past several times in the rented car. He had decided his own vehicle would not enhance his image as a mendicant cleric. His Roman collar was not as uncomfortable as he would have thought. The damned things had always struck him as chokers, Adam'sapple slicers. He found it cool—in several senses. His hair, in less worldly array, lay flat upon his head. At least in the rear-view mirror his eyes looked less decadent. Would you buy a used car from this man? His eyes crinkled. Mendax felt moved by confidence in himself. He would have made a good minister at that. It was an old thought, one that he had often had when he was flogging those goddam pamphlets. Anima Mundi. It seemed an argument for Providence that the old scheme should now, belatedly, be vindicating his faith in it.

Marge had managed to find a copy of the pamphlet the Lowry woman had professed to find so salutary. Mendax flipped through it, curious. Nothing. Vague talk of prophecies. Nostradamus, Malachy, most of it vague. Maybe at seventy-five you could supply the details yourself. All you needed as stimulus was a shudder of apprehension. The end of the world. Maybe there was consolation to be had, when death drew near, from the thought that everybody else would get theirs too, maybe in one fell blow.

What bothered Mendax was that he had come on a wild-goose chase in response to a senile letter. He had tried to laugh the letter away. Fifty thousand dollars. Did donors lay it on the line like that? He did not know. Of course it could be mere delusions of grandeur. She might have an attic full of Klondike gold certificates she hoped to bequeath in exchange for prayers. Celestial insurance. A scheme began to shape itself in Mendax's fertile mind, but he shook it away. First things first. The bird in the hand.

There had been no way he could check on the woman without jeopardizing the deal if it was genuine. A hundred miles each way. Was he willing to gamble a day to see if there really was fifty thousand dollars to be had for the asking in Fox River, Illinois? Anthony Mendax did not have it in him to turn away from odds like those. He picked up a dicky and clerical collar in a church-goods store, having them gift wrapped, a present for a friend of the cloth. The salesman to whom he gave this chatty information seemed unimpressed by Mendax's generosity.

"Is he an elderly man, sir?"

"About your age."

The salesman thought about that, as Mendax had thought he might. Snooty bastard. Mendax could not himself put an age on the skeletal clerk. Thin bald head, sunken cheeks, maybe a hundred and ten pounds wringing wet in holy water.

"Not many wear these any more."

"My friend is a conservative."

Large yellow teeth appeared as the man's lips stretched in a smile. "God bless him."

There were two Lowrys in the book, James and Mrs. August. Was James a relative? Mendax, not yet wearing the clerical collar, stopped a lovely blonde who emerged from the building.

"Pardon me. Is that the Crestview?"

She gave him a look. "Just like the sign says."

"I'm looking for James Lowry."

"Oh?" She stopped and looked him over. "Is he expecting you?"

"He may not even know me," Mendax said in a tone that suggested Ripley had not recorded all the incredible phenomena in the world.

"Is something wrong with your teeth?"

"My teeth?" Mendax glared at her. He was inordinately proud of his teeth. He had been nearly thirty when he could afford an orthodontist and he had gone for two years with a smile that looked like a bicycle wheel. The results had been worth it, though. Who did this broad think she was?

"I mean, he has dropped his practice."

"Are you sure?" Mendax lay a hand gingerly on his jaw.

"Positive."

"When did he retire?"

Her laugh was a tinkling derisive one. "He doesn't know the meaning of the word. Sorry."

Her passage to the curb demanded a drum accompaniment. She inserted herself in a lemon yellow Triumph. Mendax returned to his rented car and sat behind the wheel. He should have asked the girl if she knew Sylvia Lowry. No. That would have been a mistake. In retrospect, he approved his side of the strange exchange on the walk in front of the Crestview.

He drove to the address of Mrs. August Lowry, which tallied with that she had put in her letter. He drove past the house several times before parking across the street. He felt a renewal of doubt. The house looked like big money, like prestige. But, as it always had at crucial times in his past, doubt gave way to a sense of destiny. Mendax drove to the corner, made a U turn, and swung into the driveway leading him up to the house.

A screen door, the inner door open. Mendax stood for a moment consulting his address book, then tapped on the frame of the door. He had heard a movement within the house before he knocked, so he was playing to an imagined audience of one little old lady anxious to donate fifty thousand dollars to the work of the religious society represented by Reverend Anthony Mendax. What he fancied was an other-worldly look had taken possession of his features as he waited with Christian patience for his knock to be answered.

A minute went by. There was not another sound from within. Mendax stepped back a pace and ran a finger under his clerical collar. Couldn't she see it? It was a hot day at that. Smiling slightly, forgiving the delay, yet busy too—the work of the Lord is a demanding work—he rapped again on the door. Turn the other knuckle.

"Yes?"

It was a man's voice. Mendax felt his heart sink. He peered at the mesh of the door, but the sun lying upon it made it opaque.

"Mrs. Lowry, please."

"Come in."

The door opened and, framed in it as in a mocking mirror, stood a priest.

"Good afternoon. I'm Roger Dowling."

"Good afternoon. I hope nothing is wrong."

"Wrong?"

"Has something happened to Mrs. Lowry?"

"Come in out of the heat, Father." The priest stepped aside and Mendax had no choice but to step inside. His impulse was to dash for his car and get the hell out of there. Or was this merely a gathering of vultures? He looked more closely at Dowling.

"We can sit in the living room," Dowling said.

"I just wanted a word with Mrs. Lowry."

"It seems odd that this house is not air conditioned, doesn't it?" Dowling held an unlit pipe. Mendax took the chair the pipe pointed at. Dowling remained standing and Mendax felt immediately at a disadvantage.

"I don't believe we've met."

Mendax managed a smile. "You're local, I suppose."

"I am pastor of Saint Hilary's."

"And of course Mrs. Lowry is a parishioner."

"That's right."

But it was difficult to assess his apparent adversary. The priest, almost dapper looking even in this heat, turned his pipe in his hands as if surprised to find he was holding it. Mendax had the impression of a man almost shy, yet a glance from Dowling was more probing than a stare. Mendax felt distinctly uncomfortable in his Roman collar. It was one thing to con an old lady, quite another to deceive a man of the cloth. Or try to deceive. This bird Dowling gave the unsettling impression of seeing right through Mendax's disguise.

"You're acquainted with Mrs. Lowry?" Dowling asked.

"Not personally, no."

"Ah."

"She has written to me."

"And where are you from, Father?"

"Dubuque."

"Dubuque!" Mendax might have just picked Dowling's favorite city. "Archbishop Byrne."

Mendax smiled. He had no idea who the archbishop of Dubuque was. He did not know if Dubuque had an archbishop. Dowling, oddly self-conscious, drew a tobacco pouch from his pocket and plunged the bowl of his pipe into it.

"When did Sylvia last write you?"

It was a split second before Mendax connected the name with Mrs. Lowry. He sat forward in not wholly feigned anxiety.

"Father, has something happened to her?"

"Why would you think so?"

"Well, after all, here you are."

Dowling smiled. "If a priest, then disaster?"

"Isn't that often the case?"

"Of course, of course." Dowling looked rueful "She seems to have gone away."

"Away!"

Mendax had the sudden certainty that Sylvia Lowry was even now in Kenosha asking for him. He had made the trip in vain. He clapped a hand against his forehead.

"I was afraid of that."

"You were?"

"I have found," Mendax said, rising as he did so, "that

just dropping in unannounced is a poor way to see old friends. I was passing through town and . . ." He tossed a hand in a helpless gesture.

"Then you know the family."

"No, I don't."

"You didn't say when you had last heard from Sylvia."

Mendax could feel her letter against his breast. "I'm not sure."

"The reason I ask . . ." Dowling struck a match and puffed at his pipe. ". . . if . . ." Puff. Puff. ". . . if it would cast any light on her whereabouts, it would be very helpful."

"But I had expected to see her here."

"Of course." Dowling did not impede his passage to the door but Mendax felt he was escaping. "Are you on your way back to Dubuque?"

Mendax nodded enigmatically.

"Would you like me to tell Sylvia you called?"

"I'd appreciate that. Father Winter."

"My, what a lovely day," Dowling said. He came out onto the porch. "But so hot. Did you drive through the rain?"

"No. Actually, I came south from Milwaukee."

Dowling let him go. And that is how Mendax thought of it. It was a relief to get into the car, though it must have been close to a hundred degrees inside. He started the motor, waved at Dowling, and backed out the drive. Dowling was still standing on the porch when Mendax reached the street. He waved again, but Dowling did not return the gesture.

A block away he tore the clerical collar from his neck. A whole goddam day wasted.

12

WHEN he had gone back inside the house, Roger Dowling jotted down the license number of the car and resumed looking around the house. He wondered if Winter would even have come to the door if Dowling's car had been in the driveway instead of parked across the street. A curious man. An insufficiently curious man. Why hadn't he asked where Sylvia had gone? Why hadn't he been more persistent in asking what in the world Dowling was doing in the house if she was gone? And to say she was gone might have meant only to the corner. Winter had immediately assumed it meant on a far journey. Had he even taken it as a euphemism for a more definitive leave-taking? Winter's major interest after he entered the house had been to get out of it again.

So it had turned out to be right to answer the door. Roger Dowling had felt like an apprehended thief when he heard the sound of the car in the drive. He had expected it to be Sharon or her husband, perhaps Jimmy Lowry, someone who would have been rightfully surprised to find a priest wandering about the Lowry house.

His wandering had given him no clue as to where Sylvia Lowry might have gone. What did he expect to find that the others had not, the police, her family? The only surprise was the rosary hung over the bedpost. Beautiful beads, a silver crucifix. The phone on the bedside table would be the one on which she had called him at three in the morning. On that occasion he had urged her to say her beads. But he had already known of her devotion to the rosary. If she were at all typical, she would have a favorite rosary, if indeed she had several, and the one she used at night would surely be her favorite. Father Dowling felt certain that if Sylvia had planned to take a trip she would have taken this rosary with her.

On the other hand, it preserved the pattern. A hasty departure, unplanned, unpremeditated, into her car and off to O'Hare and then to God knew where. That she should have forgotten her rosary in such a headlong leave-taking scarcely changed the picture. The poor woman.

The phone began to ring and Dowling lurched, even more apprehensive than he had been downstairs when he heard Winter's car in the drive. He had to get out of here. But as he went downstairs the phone continued to ring. Is there anything more urgent than a ringing telephone? He went into the kitchen and picked up the extension there.

"Yes."

"Father Dowling!" It was Keegan.

"Yes, it is."

"I thought so."

"What do you mean?"

"Several neighbors have called about a strange priest lurking about."

"Well, well."

"When the squad car gets there, tell them to contact me."

"All right."

"Did you find anything?"

"That is a strange question."

"Well, you're a strange priest. All the neighbors think so. *Did* you find anything?"

"Only her rosary."

"So."

"It seems another proof that she left in a hurry. I think the squad car has arrived."

"Don't hang up, Roger. Let them in and I'll talk to them by phone."

The policeman squinting on the sunny stoop, leather and metal, an official air, looked suspiciously at Father Dowling when he came to the door.

"Chief Keegan is on the kitchen phone. He wants to talk to you."

"Keegan?"

"In here."

Warily the young patrolman came inside. His partner had remained in the car from which the crackle of a radio came as if the audible heat of the day.

"Giorgio," he said into the phone. He listened, doubt left him, he began to nod. "Right, yes, roger, okay." He handed the phone to Dowling. "We'll be going, Father."

"That was my second interruption," Dowling said to Keegan.

"What was the first?"

"A strange priest," Dowling said with emphasis.

13

THE FOLLOWING day Dowling learned the body of Sylvia Lowry had been found, lying on her kitchen floor.

"Good heavens! When had she returned?" They were in the study at St. Hilary's. Across the desk from him, Phil Keegan was sipping a beer.

"She hadn't. She died three days ago."

"How is that possible?"

"She froze to death."

"I don't understand."

"It took us a while to figure it out too. The body of Sylvia Lowry has spent part of the past three days in the freezer chest in her basement."

Dowling felt horror and disbelief and impatience. "You said she was found on the kitchen floor."

"With a nasty gash in her head. At first it seemed simple. Well, not simple. She had been struck by something quite heavy, the blow had killed her. There were indications, from the position of the body, that that's what had happened. And then we have a curve thrown at us by the coroner. The body had been frozen and then thawed out. Do you know Morton, the coroner?" Keegan twirled a finger around one ear in a gesture Dowling had not seen in decades. "But he was serious. Where else but in the freezer? The chest was empty, no food in it, and there was blood. Sylvia Lowry's blood."

"God rest her soul."

"If she wasn't dead, she must have been unconscious when he put her in there."

"He?"

"Someone carried her downstairs. She was a small woman but even so . . ."

"And three days later carried her up again?"

Keegan nodded.

Dowling thought of the frail little woman, beset by fears, afraid to be alone, fearful of death. Her worst fears had been realized. He prayed that her end had not been too dreadful, that unconsciousness had intervened. He thought of the reiterated prayer when she said her beads, the words of the Ave, pray for us sinners, now and at the hour of our death, and he hoped her plea had been heard. At any rate, she was now safely on the other side of the grave. On this side still was the poor sinner who had murdered her, struck her, and then stuffed her into a freezer. He did not want to think of the possibility of her regaining consciousness in that dark cold place, fulfilling the dreadful recurrent dream of waking in one's own grave.

"To think I was wandering about her house yesterday."

"So was I. It wouldn't have mattered if we had found her, Father. She was already dead. What time did you leave the house yesterday?"

"Shortly after I spoke with you on the phone. Five or ten minutes later."

"About two."

"How long had the body been out of the freezer when it was found?"

"Long enough to thaw out completely."

"When was she found?"

"This morning."

"Who found the body?"

"We did. We got an anonymous call."

"Saying what?"

"Sylvia Lowry is in her kitchen."

"A man or woman caller?"

"A man. Now, what did you mean yesterday about being interrupted by a strange priest?"

"I have the number of his car. An Illinois license, though he claimed to live in Dubuque and to have just driven from Milwaukee."

"Is that what you meant by strange?"

"I don't think he was a priest."

"Why?"

"It's not as conclusive as it would have been a few years ago, but he wore a ring, he had a mustache and side-burns. He was a very vain man."

Keegan was unimpressed by these as bases for doubting the man was a priest. "We'll check out the car."

"How is the family taking this?"

Keegan shrugged. Dowling lit his pipe.

"You don't suspect them?"

"Of killing their mother?"

"She was afraid of them."

"Do you have a favorite suspect?"

Dowling looked out the window. Did he seriously suspect someone? Of course he knew Phil Keegan did not find it incredible that a mother might be murdered by her children. They had talked sufficiently of such matters to learn that neither retained much ability to be surprised by what men do. If there is any surprise about murder it is that anyone is capable of it. It was nonsense to speak of the murderer as a type. That was like thinking of sinners as a portion of humanity. Keegan knew better than Dowling that most murders are intramural: brother kills or is killed by sister, parent by child, husband by wife. It is rare that one is murdered by a stranger or indeed by a non-relative.

"We'll get him," Keegan said grimly.

"Or her."

"Why do you say that?"

"You haven't excluded a female assailant, have you?"

"I haven't excluded anyone."

"Not even me?"

Keegan made a face.

"Now, Phil, be professional. I was lurking around the house."

"Motive?"

"Money."

"Are you in her will?"

"Have you inquired at her bank, by the way?"

"What do you mean?"

Dowling waved his hand. "She had been harassing me with dead-of-night phone calls. I was enraged." He stopped. "The car."

"What about it?"

"Who parked it at O'Hare?"

"We don't know."

"You don't know."

Keegan got up. "What will I learn from her banker?"

"That she had something on the order of one hundred and fifty thousand dollars in cash at home. That is a reasonable assumption. She took it from her safety deposit box."

"One hundred and fifty thousand! That's motive enough for anybody."

And so no doubt it was. Some poor soul had risked damnation for a good deal more than thirty pieces of silver. The bargain was still an infinitely bad one. The attack on Sylvia must have been premeditated; a rather bizarre plan had emerged. And there had to be some advantage to the killer to gain three days before the body was discovered. Someone had killed Sylvia and then made it look as if she had simply gone away.

Dowling stopped these thoughts. Slowly, slowly. The inference was inviting but not compelling. Had it been the same person who put Sylvia's body into the freezer and then removed it sometime later?

14

JIMMY LOWRY'S apartment, a glass aerie overlooking Fox River, was what, Father Dowling thought, is often referred to as a bachelor's pad. The dominant colors were red and white. A white carpet, its pile ankle deep but strange and stringy too, like the coat of some animal. Puffy misshapen furniture of red patent leather was scattered about on the peltlike carpet, with occasional tables of glass and stainless steel. An ell of walls were windows; the other two, one white, one red, displayed no pictures. Father Dowling moved with a sense of wading toward the windowed walls and the view of the city.

"Just make yourself comfortable, Father," Jimmy Lowry called from offstage.

Comfortable? Dowling smiled. Had this been the scene of orgies of abandonment? No doubt. He had few delusions about such matters. Squalor or sumptuousness, the setting in which the human soul enacted its drama was surprisingly unimportant. He had known wealthy men of genuine poverty of spirit and beggars whose souls were riddled with avarice and greed. Of course it was unlikely that purity of heart would survive this warren in the sky where Jimmy Lowry dwelt.

"You were trained as a dentist, I'm told."

"That's right." A serious, tight-lipped Jimmy bobbed his head. "University of Illinois."

"Did you practice here in town?"

"My offices were downstairs in this building."

"What did your mother think of that?"

The question was intentionally ambiguous. Jimmy looked at Dowling and the priest saw a quip die in the younger man's eyes.

"Sharon would tell you she was deeply disappointed in me for dropping my practice."

"She being your mother."

"Yes."

"And what would you tell me?"

Jimmy lit a filter-tip cigarette. He exhaled a great cloud of smoke, open-mouthed.

"What is this, Father? Do you want me to feel guilty for my mother's death, the cause of her loneliness, the boy who broke her heart?"

"Good heavens, why should I want that?"

"Because guilt is your stock in trade. Get a person to feel guilty and you can get a hook into him."

"You make guilt sound like something I invented."

Jimmy smiled. "Look, Father, I don't want to hassle about religion. But I don't want to talk about how I disappointed my mother either."

"Of course. That isn't why I came."

Jimmy opened his hands, receptive.

"You'll be taking care of the funeral arrangements, I imagine?"

"Me?" Jimmy was surprised. "I thought Bill."

"It's really not all that complicated. But one of you will have to go there. If only to insure that your mother doesn't go to her grave in a ten-thousand-dollar coffin."

"That much?" Jimmy's brow raised.

"It's possible to spend more."

"The crooks."

"Actually, many people insist on what they think the best."

"Under gentle pressure? Yes, I suppose I'll take care of things."

"McGinnis is the undertaker most frequently involved in funerals at Saint Hilary's."

"Aha. A little kickback?"

"He provides our parish calendar," Dowling said, unperturbed. "And he knew your family."

"I know McGinnis. Poor Mother," Jimmy said suddenly. His face relaxed and he looked his age. "What a way to go. She was such a fastidious person, and to think of her being carted up and down stairs like that, well . . ."

"Death is seldom dignified."

"I guess not. Did you know her well?"

"Not really. I haven't been at Saint Hilary's all that long."

"But she confided in you."

Dowling did not answer, just looked expressionlessly at Jimmy.

"Called you up in the middle of the night."

"I wondered if you had been told about that."

"Why wouldn't I be told?"

"I didn't mean it that way."

"What was she scared of, Father?"

"Nothing. Everything. She was old and alone and afraid of death."

"Just death? Sharon said Mother told you she was afraid of us."

"What could she have possibly meant?"

"Well, look what happened."

Dowling looked at Jimmy. "Yes. I see what you mean."

Jimmy adopted a sage expression, the knowledgeable veteran of the world's underside, but Dowling saw only a confused middle-aged man who probably did not yet admit to himself he was middle-aged. How sad this apartment was with its joyless evanescence, its assertive vulgarity. Father Dowling suspected they were not alone. Jimmy had rather definitively shut the door leading off this room and the priest had thought he heard sounds of another's presence. Was it to Jimmy's credit that he was embarrassed because his other guest was making herself known? There seemed little doubt it was a girl. Well, thought Father Dowling, there are worse things. The weakness of the flesh seemed almost innocent compared with the brutal killing of Sylvia Lowry.

"You're not shocked by the thought that her own family might have wanted my mother dead?"

"Not many things shock a priest."

"How about the suggestion of a drink before lunch?" Jimmy went toward his plastic bar, sliding across the carpet in his moccasins.

"Not even that. But no thanks."

"I'm having one. How about coffee?"

"Don't bother."

"It's no bother." Jimmy's look became defiant. He crossed to the closed door and opened it. "Hey, Martha."

There was a long silence.

"Martha!"

"What is it?" A voice groping for a proper tone.

"How about making some coffee, okay?"

"Okay."

She came into the room wearing a robe, no pretense there, but her eyes managed not to meet Dowling's.

"Don't make coffee just for me," Dowling said.

"That's all right. I haven't had breakfast yet."

"These are confusing events." Dowling got off the plastic chair he had been seated in and followed the girl toward the kitchen, which was separated from the living area by a counter with stools. "Did you know Mrs. Lowry well, Martha?"

"No," the girl said. She looked at Jimmy. "I was never introduced to her."

"My name is Roger Dowling. Mrs. Lowry lived in my parish."

"This is Martha Nagy," Jimmy said grudgingly.

Unexpectedly, the girl thrust her hand out. Dowling shook it gravely. He had the uneasy feeling that, in her eyes, he was conferring some sort of semi-benediction on this ménage.

"I'm going to have to make the arrangements," Jimmy said. "For the funeral."

"Why you?"

"What do you mean, why me?"

"I don't mean anything. I just thought that Bill . . ."

"I am her son," Jimmy said. "Bill is her son-in-law."

"And I," she said, with a bright vacant smile before turning her back on him, "am Martha."

"Was William Cordwill your mother's lawyer?"

"Bill? No."

"I see." Dowling behaved as if an important line of conversation had been cut off by Jimmy's reply.

"Do I need a lawyer to make arrangements for the funeral?"

"Hardly. Your mother may have had burial insurance."

"There is a family plot. McGinnis will know all about that. My father . . ."

"Yes. I never knew him."

"He was a great man."

"I have heard only good things of him."

"That is where my mother went wrong, making a habit of missing him. Her life had been lived in the shadow of his. She never adjusted to being alone. She wouldn't travel, she wouldn't do things. She wanted to die, I think. And she insisted on staying on in that big house all by herself." Jimmy shook his head. "It's a terrible thing to say, but sometimes I think she expected a violent end, even prayed for it."

"Jimmy!"

He ignored Martha. She had put a cup of instant coffee on the counter for Dowling.

"It was foolish of her to live alone in that house."

"But why would anyone kill her?" Dowling asked. "'What did he have to gain?"

"Gain? Read the papers, Father. People kill for a dollar bill or a cheap watch. They beat in old people's heads for an empty purse or for a wallet they know won't hold enough money to justify their trouble."

Dowling nodded in sad agreement.

"Drugs," Jimmy said. "We're a nation of hopheads. And how are they going to get the stuff except by stealing?"

"Was anything missing from your mother's house?"

"I'm not talking about my mother."

"But you think it may have been a thief who killed her?"

"How would I know?"

"But, Jimmy, you said . . ."

He turned to Martha. "Look, why don't you make breakfast like a good girl. I've got things to do."

"Yes, master."

"Come on. This has hit me pretty hard."

Even Dowling was startled by this remark. Was it unfair to see it as a theatric bid for compliance from Martha? Dowling tasted the coffee and got off his stool.

"I must run."

He thanked Martha for the coffee. Jimmy came with him to the door.

"McGinnis. I'll call him as soon as I've eaten."

Jimmy still held a glass and his breath was heavy with whisky. The grieving son? Perhaps. In the elevator Dowling dropped swiftly to street level. It was good to have his feet on the ground again.

15

THE CORDWILL house was grave and quiet. Bill Cordwill admitted Father Dowling with a doleful expression, speaking in a whisper.

"Sharon is taking this pretty badly."

"Of course."

"Have you seen the newspaper?"

Dowling nodded. It must be especially painful for Sharon to read of her mother as the frozen corpse, the icebox murder. The *Tribune* was relatively tasteful but the *Sun-Times* showed a typical lack of restraint. Sylvia Lowry's going was merely another occasion to titillate the jaded urban reader.

"How long will they keep it up?"

"That's hard to say. It may be over now. Until they catch the murderer."

"And then a trial." Bill Cordwill passed a hand over the pasty expanse of his face. He had not shaved and his eyes were puffy and red. His breath smelled of liquor, but it was an old smell, not the fresh redolence of Jimmy's half an hour ago.

"The police will be discreet."

"The police. I still can't believe this, Father. Sylvia Lowry murdered. What kind of a world is this?"

It would not be kind in the circumstances to say it was the same kind of world it had always been. Murder, mayhem, rape, theft, injustice: it was perhaps tempting to certain ideologies to regard these as either recent arrivals on the historical scene or as receding relics of an unenlightened time. Alas, they were permanent features of the human drama, not correctible malfunctions, not if correction meant tinkering from outside with the human machine. Dowling was no more attracted by the ideal of justice that guided Phil Keegan and, he supposed, Bill Cordwill too when he expressed the hope, as they went through the house to the kitchen, that the police would do their business quickly. Apprehension? Punishment? That was not the essential thing. Far more important was the spiritual condition of the one who had killed Sylvia Lowry. He—or she—must recognize the sinfulness of what had been done, ask God's pardon for the deed, repent. Above all, the doer must be protected from the suggestion that he could not have acted otherwise, that something in his psyche or surroundings or genes or upbringing explained the action. Better an unapprehended murderer who knew what he had done and was genuinely sorry before God, than a caught culprit condemned to years of thought control as he was programmed for re-entry into society by technicians who regarded him as a machine.

A teen-aged girl was in the kitchen when they entered.

"My daughter, Cheryl. Father Dowling."

"Good morning, Cheryl. I'm so sorry about your grandmother."

The girl nodded, flattered to be treated as the center of tragedy.

"I shall remember her in my Mass at noon."

"I've lost my faith," the girl announced, her chin lifting.

Father Dowling smiled. "Then I shall remember you as well."

Bill Cordwill was embarrassed by his daughter's candor. His expression tried to elicit from Father Dowling the unstated agreement that Cheryl was going through a stage, that a loss of faith was an adolescent drama that had to play itself out. Dowling's expression was as enigmatic as an Easter Island idol.

"Pour Father some coffee, Cheryl." Cordwill had stopped whispering now that they were in the kitchen.

"I've already spoken with Jimmy," Dowling said to Cordwill. They sat at the table with mugs of coffee before them. "He will make the arrangements."

"Jimmy?"

"I suggested McGinnis."

"Of course. Jimmy can be very efficient when he wants to be."

"He tells me he is no longer practicing dentistry."

"That's right."

Cheryl, holding a mug of coffee in both hands, stood with her back to the stove, watching the two men at the table. She seemed to find the tableau amusing.

She said, "According to the paper, Grandma was taken from her basement yesterday to thaw out."

"Cheryl," Cordwill barked. He was genuinely angry.

"But aren't we all suspects?"

"That isn't a damned bit funny."

"Even I am a suspect," Dowling agreed. "I was in the house on Tuesday."

"What for?"

Dowling smiled apologetically at Cordwill. "Curiosity, I'm afraid. I told myself I was going there as her concerned pastor, but the fact is I was trying to understand how she could have just run away as she apparently had."

"And all the while," Cheryl said wondrously. Her father glared at her.

"All the while she was down in the basement," Dowling said. "But why would anyone have looked for her there, and in the freezer?"

"Why would anyone put her there?" Cheryl joined them at the table.

"To preserve her?"

Cordwill pushed away from the table slightly, perhaps to signal his disapproval of this ghoulish exchange between Dowling and his daughter.

"But why?"

"That is the question."

"And of course to hide her. That way, for three days, she was just a missing person, not someone who had been murdered."

"And then she was taken out again."

"Now, that's what mystifies me," Cheryl said. "First he wants to hide her or hide the fact there has been a murder. Now he wants it known."

"He?"

Cheryl looked surprised. She had her mother's, and her grandmother's, clear eyes. Cordwill had returned his elbows to the table.

"Not a man?"

"Is it necessary that it be a man?"

Cheryl nodded approvingly. "Of course it could be a woman. Grandma was not all that heavy. *I* could have carried her."

Her father was staring at her, shocked, horrified.

"She would have been quite heavy," Dowling said.

"Dead weight," Cheryl agreed.

Her father protested. "Stop it, Cheryl. This is not a game. We are talking of your grandmother."

"Who has been murdered, Daddy. And, as Father Dowling agrees, we are all suspects. Now, where was I this time yesterday? In bed. Mama was on the golf course, where else? And you were at the office."

Cordwill made a despairing sound, but his daughter went on.

"Those are our stories, anyway. But the police will want to know how I can prove I was still in bed. Who else was home? No one. So couldn't I have gone to Grandma's, dragged her up to the kitchen, come back here and been ostensibly in bed when you dashed in?"

Father Dowling did not wholly disapprove of Cordwill's stopping the girl. Cheryl was taking a kind of pleasure from her speculation that was quite inappropriate. When she had been sent from the room by her irate father, the two men sat silently over their coffee.

"Kids," Cordwill said.

"Was she close to her grandmother?"

"Not lately. She used to be."

"Of course Sylvia must have changed in recent years."

"That's putting it mildly. You should have known her when her husband was still alive. Now, there was a man, August Lowry. Sylvia drew vitality from the man, moon to his sun. She was vibrant, energetic, a real force in the city. And then he died and she became, well, what she became. A whining old woman, sniveling in church, afraid of everything."

"How did he die?"

"August? His heart gave out."

"At home?"

Cordwill smiled despite himself. "On the golf course. Sharon predicts that is where she will die too. Between the tee and the green, most likely in the rough. With her spikes on." He got rid of the smile. "She is under sedation."

"Had she drifted away from her mother too?"

"It was Sylvia who drifted away."

"Then it was the father, August, who kept the family close?"

"That's right."

"Sharon took his death hard too?"

Cordwill hesitated, then leaned forward. He was whispering again. "Very hard. Extremely hard."

Dowling nodded.

"Call it a nervous breakdown. It was touch and go there for the better part of a year. I don't think there is any danger of a repetition, but I didn't want to take the chance. I had the doctor here last night. That's why the sedatives. Normally she wouldn't need them. You know her. How many women her age are as healthy?"

"Do you golf?"

"If you can call it that. Incidentally, I'm glad you asked Jimmy to take care of things. It's about time he assumed some family responsibility. I did everything when his father died."

"Did Jimmy take it hard?"

"In his way."

"Meaning?"

"That's when he left his wife. It was as if his father's death relieved him of all his obligations. He divorced Harriet, closed his office, became a real wheeler-dealer. I sometimes think he is trying to match his father's success."

"Has he?"

"Who knows?"

"Did he have children?"

"One. A boy. Retarded. They put him away."

"And what happened to his wife?"

"She remarried."

It was like hearing in a more casual way one of those cases he had anguished over for so many years. If the woman, Harriet, was Catholic she was now locked in an illicit marriage—if her marriage to Jimmy had been valid. If the playboy he now was had been latent in him when he married, had he really meant it when he repeated the marriage vows or had he intended to be unfaithful, a hedonist, once the opportunity presented itself? The slightest objective proof of that and the fat would be in the fire, or out of the fire, so far as Jimmy's ex-wife was concerned. Would she care? Would it matter to her? Dowling had no illusions about the seriousness with which the world took the Church's marriage laws. He knew they seemed quaintly archaic, legalistic chains or simply unrealistic, since even Catholics, in the crunch, ignored them in practice and then contested them before the marriage tribunal.

"And Jimmy has not married again?"

Cordwill adopted a gnomic look. "No."

"I met Martha this morning."

"You did?"

Father Dowling had the impression that Bill Cordwill wished to apologize for his brother-in-law.

16

HER MOTHER lay in drugged sleep, mouth open, hair every which way on the pillow. The tanned skin looked lined and old in relaxation. Cheryl stood beside the bed wondering if in her dreams her mother mourned Grandma. It was no secret that Grandma had shunned them for more than a year. Why? Why not? Mom, Dad, Uncle Jimmy and his girl: Grandma had not wanted to know any more about them than she had to. Not that she hadn't tried to pump Cheryl when she visited; it had been that subtle grilling which put a stop to those visits. Cheryl had not wanted to inform on her family. Squealing to Grandma. And to God.

"What Mass did you go to this morning?"

"We didn't go."

"Did you go last night? Saturday-evening Mass counts for Sunday now." The old woman's smile had pleaded for a lie or for a different truth than the one Cheryl could give her.

"Do you really go every day?"

"I try to, yes. It's hardly an accomplishment, Cheryl. What else do I have to do?" But Grandma had shocked herself. "I don't mean that Mass is where one goes when there is nothing else to do. We have a new pastor."

"What do you do all day?"

"I putter about the house. I read." She paused. "I say my prayers. I pray for all of you, for my children, for my grandchildren. That is what old ladies are for, I guess. When I am gone you must pray for me."

Remembering that now, in her own room, dressed, Cheryl looked out the window. Prayer. What was it but mumbling words to yourself? Where is Grandma now, she wondered. She closed her eyes, closed them tight, and thought of Grandma. Had she simply stopped being, become nothing at all, or was she still going on somewhere, in heaven?

Cheryl opened her eyes and picked up a brush from her dresser. Stroking her hair, she thought of heaven. She had never been able to understand heaven. It was where one would be happy forever and ever, but no one seemed to know what you did there. You won't want to do anything. It won't be like time. You'll see God. Well, if there was that little to do in heaven, and if Grandma was there, it would be just more of what her life had been, a lot more. Of course she could go on praying there. For her children and for her grandchildren.

Cheryl threw back her head and looked at the ceiling. She imagined her grandma up there somewhere, invisible, but able to see her. And she was asking God to look after Cheryl.

That was a pleasant thought. Cheryl liked the idea that there was someone up there speaking on her behalf.

Could Grandma see the one who had killed her? Would she be praying for her murderer, praying he got caught? Who was he?

Cheryl stopped brushing her hair. She could hear the low voices of her father and the priest in the kitchen. Father Dowling had agreed they were all suspects. Maybe Uncle Jimmy had killed Grandma.

She watched her eyes widen in the mirror. Uncle Jimmy had a reputation for irresponsibility, and of course he was silly about women. He went with a woman for a month or two, she actually would stay with him in his apartment, and then, before you knew it, there was a different one. How did he manage it? What dopes those women must be, letting Jimmy use them and then throw them aside for a replacement. How cruel and selfish. And he was such an ass, acting like a kid, dressing like a young man. He had an annoying way of talking to Cheryl as if they were allies against the grown-up world, but she always had the impression that he was speaking to be overheard, that his words weren't meant for her alone. She always laughed and let him kid around, but she did not like him. She did not trust him either. He could have killed Grandma, easy. But why would he?

Well, why did he treat women the way he did? Why had he divorced Aunt Harriet and abandoned little Arthur, who was retarded and had been put away somewhere, no one seemed to be sure where. When Cheryl suggested once that they ought to visit her cousin—he was, after all, their flesh and blood—there had been an uncomfortable silence. Her father said she might ask Uncle Jimmy if he would take her along the next time he visited Arthur.

"Can't be done, sweetheart. They wouldn't let you in."

"Why not?"

"It's that kind of place, I'm afraid." It was obvious he was lying. It was obvious he did not want to talk about it.

"They'd have to let me in. I'm his cousin. Uncle Jimmy, I want to see him. Please."

"We'll see, Cheryl."

It was such an obvious putdown that Cheryl had wanted to cry. Of course she would not cry. But while she was trying not to, Uncle Jimmy escaped. She never mentioned it to him again. Arthur was another reason Grandma had drawn away from Jimmy and all of them.

"In an institution," the old woman said, her voice shocked. "A Lowry in a public institution. There is absolutely no excuse for that. Public institutions are for people who cannot pay."

"My father says we pay for public institutions with our taxes."

"Hmph. Our taxes pay for the jails too. Does he plan to spend time there to get his money's worth?"

"I hardly remember Arthur," Cheryl said.

"Oh, he was an angel. They are called special children, Cheryl, and they are. They are close to God. He loves them in a way we will never understand."

"Why?"

"Because they are innocent. They are the only human beings who cannot sin."

"I never thought of that."

"Do you know what I like to think?"

"What?"

"That deep inside, in a way they can't express, their minds are clear, much clearer than ours."

"Do you really think so?"

"It could be true, Cheryl."

"I suppose."

The trouble was that so many other things could be true and weren't. Cheryl believed in God if only because her grandma wanted her to so badly. She also liked to come back from visits to Grandma Lowry's and talk about going to Mass every day at noon and saying the rosary together at night.

"Grandma says we should do that here," Cheryl reported.

"Yes, we should," her mother agreed.

"She's right," her father said.

But they never said the rosary, they never said grace at meals, and they very seldom even went to Mass. That wasn't right and Cheryl knew it. No wonder Grandma had been so disappointed in them.

But she was a lot more disappointed in Uncle Jimmy, so he must be the one who killed Grandma. How would the police find that out? Uncle Jimmy was so sneaky they would never catch him. If the police were ever going to know, someone was going to have to tell them. That was when Cheryl decided to send the letter.

She knew exactly how to do this, of course; she had seen it in movies and on TV. She snipped letters and sometimes whole words from the paper, pasted the message on a sheet of paper from her father's desk, used one of the plain envelopes her mother kept in the kitchen, and mailed it several blocks away from home. She had the feeling, riding back on her bicycle, that Grandma Lowry knew what she had done and was glad.

17

GENE turned on the bedside radio that morning, waking her, and when she complained said he wanted to hear the weather report. But the news came first and Edna Hospers was jolted fully awake by the report of the death of Mrs. Lowry.

"Mrs. Lowry! Did you hear?"

But Gene had heard. He motioned her to keep quiet so they could hear it all. Edna could not believe it. Mrs. Lowry had been found dead in her home. Police were investigating. And then there was a lot about Mrs. Lowry's late husband, a prominent member of the Fox River community, etc. etc.

"The police," Edna said. "Good grief, do you suppose some thief got in and . . ."

"Maybe there's more in the paper."

There was a photograph of the body being carried from the Lowry house, but it was zipped up in some sort of bag and strapped to a shallow basketlike stretcher.

"She was such a tiny woman, Gene." Tears started up in her eyes, she couldn't help it. She didn't want to alarm the children and have them ask questions. They would remember Sylvia. But she did not want to explain death to them, not today.

"How did she die?" she asked Gene, keeping her voice down but unable to control a half sob.

"She got hit on the head."

"Oh!"

She put the kids in the playroom, letting them eat their breakfast on the little table there. It was like a party. Back in the kitchen, she read over Gene's shoulder, but in a minute he handed her the paper.

"Not much there."

"Yesterday afternoon," Edna mused.

"They're not sure, Edna."

"I wonder what I was doing when it happened?"

"What the hell difference does that make?"

"Does it have to make a difference? I just wonder."

The truth was that she was sure she'd had some kind of premonition at the moment Mrs. Lowry died, some sign. Every once in a while she would stop in the midst of what she was doing—dishes, beds, fixing a meal—and would have the eerie certainty that something or someone was trying to get through to her. She had never mentioned this to anyone, not to Gene or anyone else. There was something wrong about it, something almost sacrilegious. She had even wondered if she should mention it in confession, but she had convinced herself it was not really a sin. Besides, she couldn't help it if she had these experiences, whatever they were. But she was certain there had been nothing yesterday. A few days before—now, that was a different story.

"The last time I saw her was Sunday," Edna said.

Gene picked up his coffee.

"Isn't it funny? You would think you would have some sort of intimation the last time you saw someone alive, particularly if they were going to be killed."

"Forget it, Edna."

"I'll bet if I could remember what she said, some innocent little remark, it would mean more now than she had meant when she spoke it."

Gene got to his feet and looked down at her, shaking his head. "You're losing your marbles, Edna. Do you know that?"

"When was the last time you saw her?"

"Two minutes ago."

He pointed to the paper and her eyes dropped to the photo of the pitifully small bundle being carried away from the Lowry house. It was the last time she would leave it. Once more the tears started up in Edna's eyes.

The sound of the truck starting in the driveway surprised her. She had not even heard Gene leave the house. She ran to the door and outside, waving after him, but he did not see her. She felt terrible. Weeping over Mrs. Lowry and ignoring her own husband. I'll make it up to him, she thought. A good dinner. Steak? He loved steak. But she could not find the outdoor grill.

18

THE CAR whose number Father Dowling had given Keegan had been rented at O'Hare by a man they were having difficulty tracing through the credit card he had used.

"Was the card stolen?" Keegan asked Lieutenant Horvath.

"They're not prepared to say."

"What are they prepared to say?"

"That the card was issued to Owen Bartley of Kenosha, Wisconsin."

"So find Owen Bartley."

"I did. He's dead. He's been dead for two years."

"And still renting cars. Shame on him. Why the hell can't they just say the card is stolen?"

"Because it hasn't been reported stolen."

"Does Bartley have any heirs?"

"The Kenosha police are checking. Fellow named Rush. Remember him?"

Keegan nodded. "Good. Keep me posted. That looks like our best lead."

"What about the letter?"

"Get out of here."

The letter lay on Keegan's desk, a travesty of the paste-up letters of a million movies. Jimmy Lowry Killed His Mother. Jimmy? He was still Dr. Lowry to most people. James, Jim—but Jimmy? The thing about a letter like this was that it had the effect of exonerating Jimmy Lowry. Was he capable of putting together a clownish accusation of himself? Keegan pressed a button.

"Is Horvath still there?"

"He just left."

"Send Peanuts in here."

Peanuts was a rookie who owed his presence on the force to the fact that both his father and his brother were on the city council. Keegan kept Peanuts on because he was afraid he might run for the council too. That would really be the revenge of the Pianonnis. Peanuts came across the room to Keegan's desk, moving on the balls of his feet, arms akimbo. He had the body of a weight lifter, and a matching head.

"Take this letter to Solomon in the lab. I want him to take it seriously, Peanuts. Understand? Paper, paste, the paper it was clipped from, prints, everything."

"Yes sir." Peanuts took the letter delicately between a meaty thumb and forefinger.

"And close the door after you."

"Yes sir."

He ought to get the hell out of here for a while, go somewhere he could get a little perspective on matters. He lit a cigarette. The door opened and Peanuts's head appeared.

"There's a priest to see you, Captain. Dowling."

Keegan hesitated. He was in no mood to talk with Dowling now, but the priest almost never came here so it might be important. He indicated to Peanuts that he would see Dowling.

"Has the body been released, Phil?"

"No reason why it shouldn't be. Morton says he's through with it."

"Then the cause of death has been established?"

Keegan made a disgusted noise. "We still have our choice of causes. Maybe the blow on the head killed her; maybe it only rendered her unconscious. Morton likes the second possibility. Then he can say she froze to death in a July heat wave in Illinois. Death by freezing, complicated by lack of oxygen. I suppose it doesn't really matter."

"Could the blow to her head have happened when she was put into the freezer?"

"No. Morton is certain about that, and let's hope he's right. The alternative is pretty gruesome."

"James Lowry is taking care of things at McGinnis."

"James. Who calls him Jimmy?"

"His family all do."

"And his girl friends. Lots of others, I suppose."

"Does it matter?"

Keegan told Dowling about the letter he had received. The priest was no more impressed by it than he was.

"Got any ideas, Roger?"

"I'm very curious about Father Winter, of course."

"We're working on that. He rented the car with a credit card belonging to a man who died two years ago."

"Ah. Where did he rent the car?"

"At O'Hare."

"No wonder you're working on it. Do you suppose it's just a coincidence that Sylvia's car is found at O'Hare and that a mysterious stranger rents a car there and shows up at her house?"

Keegan shrugged. "I'm waiting to hear from the Kenosha police."

"Kenosha?"

"It's where the man whose credit card was used is buried."

"Now, wouldn't it be convenient if the alleged Father Winter is also in Kenosha and could be traced through that credit card."

" 'Lucky' would be a better word."

"And what else do you have?"

"Well, I have suspects galore. There is Jimmy Lowry. There are the Cordwills."

"All of whom can account for their whereabouts on Tuesday at the appropriate time?"

"Yes and no."

"Oh?"

"Put it this way, Roger. It is not impossible that any one of them was at the house between the time after you left and the time the body was found."

"And of course Winter could have returned."

"Right. Someone put the body in the kitchen and someone a good deal later called us to tell us it was there. The same person? Perhaps. We know a few people who might have done one or both of those things. There are no doubt a dozen more people who could have done them. From Monday on, that house was like a public building. How did you get in on Tuesday?"

"I walked in."

"There you are."

"Is it still wide open?"

"Horvath has informed the family that we are through there. He locked up when he finished."

"Whom do you mean by family?"

"Cordwill, I suppose. Why?"

"No reason. The fact that Sylvia Lowry apparently had a house full of cash is the motive?"

"Unless we are dealing with a nut, yes. Which means we need somebody who knew about the money. Which means the family. This Winter guy, suspicious as his actions are, doesn't look too promising for just that reason. How would he know of the money? Of course, if we haul him in for questioning we might find he did know. But was he ever in the house before you let him in?"

"Are there fingerprints you can't account for?"

"Lots of them. I don't have a complete report yet. Jimmy Lowry and Bill Cordwill were easy. They were both in the service. We can't get a set from Mrs. Cordwill at the moment. Even so, we will end up with lots of unidentified prints. We always do. If we find Winter, if his prints are in the house, elsewhere than in the living room where you talked with him, I'll be able to hold him. For how long? Who knows? Unless he knew about the money."

"Was there money in the house?"

"Yes."

"Did someone find it?"

"We didn't."

"It's only an inference that it was there."

"Her safety deposit box."

"Even if it's empty . . ."

"I know. I know. But we have to have a motive."

"Or a crazy man."

"You're not helping."

"Where were the members of the family on Monday?"

Keegan looked at the priest. He had never known Roger to be so persistently inquisitive. Well, after all, it was a parishioner of his who had been killed, and he had some acquaintance with the family. It would have been strange if Roger had been indifferent to what little was known of Sylvia Lowry's death. And talking it over with Dowling was almost as good as mulling it over in his own mind. Talking aloud to Horvath was a different matter. How could he conceal from Horvath his fear that they were confronted here by a puzzle they weren't going to be able to solve easily, if at all.

"Monday," he said. "First of all, what hours are important? The fact that the body was in the freezer for a good while makes things both easy and difficult for the coroner. He says. Anyway, Morton tells me not before noon on Monday. So the whole thing runs from noon on Monday until Wednesday morning when the officers responded to an anonymous call and found the body of Sylvia Lowry on her kitchen floor."

"No longer frozen."

"No longer frozen. They were not immediately convinced she was dead, as a matter of fact. Anyway, start with Monday and James Lowry. Where was he from noon onward? He had lunch with Henry Bradshaw of the bank at the Athletic Club, from twelve to one fifteen. They walked from the club to the bank, where they parted. Lowry's car was in a lot across the street from the bank. But he did go inside the bank before parting from Bradshaw."

"And?"

"And had his parking ticket stamped. That way he didn't have to pay a parking fee."

"The rich are different from you and me."

"That's why they're rich."

"I wonder who paid for the lunch."

"Bradshaw."

"Fair enough, I suppose. If they were discussing business."

"Informally."

"Which Henry Bradshaw is reluctant to discuss?"

"We haven't pressed him on it. Do you know him, Roger?"

"We've met."

"Lowry left the parking lot and drove to his apartment. There he picked up Martha Nagy; they drove to the Fox River Marina, where they boarded Lowry's boat. They spent the afternoon cruising the river. They ate aboard. They returned the boat to the marina at nine o'clock and returned to the apartment. Period."

"What does cruising the river consist of?"

"That, of course, is the point. They could have left the boat and been on land for hours."

"They?"

"One or both."

"Was he reluctant to tell you all this?"

"No. Not eager either. What he told us checks, but, as you guessed, it doesn't begin to rule him out."

"Them."

"All right. Either one."

"Where did Miss Nagy have lunch?"

"She claims to have been in bed until twelve thirty. She left the apartment for the first time that day when Lowry came back for her."

"True?"

"Nothing suggests that it isn't."

"Did you also find out what the two of them were doing on Tuesday?"

"So far this is an extremely informal inquiry. They all realize we will be getting back to them."

"Tuesday will be the most important day."

"Why do you say that?"

"If concealing the body had any purpose, it must have been to facilitate the search of the house."

"But someone who had nothing to do with Sylvia's disappearance, yet knew of the money, could have shown up at the house to look for it."

"But Sylvia has ostensibly flown away. Her car is gone. It will be found at O'Hare. One who knew of the money and who believed Sylvia had gone away would assume she had taken the money with her."

"So we have the reason for the concealment of the body. It is to throw others off the scent and to give the killer a clear track in searching the house. Whoever else might know of the money is bound to assume it has gone with Sylvia."

Dowling frowned through this summary.

Keegan said, "And when the killer found the money, he called us."

Even to say it was to reveal its implausibility. Why should the killer be so accommodating?

"There could be two, even three different people, Phil. A killer, a hunter, a caller."

"Not very likely."

"Perhaps not. But it will be interesting to know what James Lowry and his Martha were doing on Tuesday."

"And then there are the Cordwills."

Dowling was still there when the call from Casey came in. Keegan put down the phone and said, "Well, that clears that up."

Dowling looked receptive.

"It seemed pretty convenient to have an empty freezer to put the body in. We checked and found that Sylvia Lowry had stocked up with a quarter of beef and some odds and ends just two months ago. That freezer had to be unloaded."

"The meat has been found?"

"People on the west side began complaining about an odor and about dogs by day and raccoons by night. It was Sylvia Lowry's meat. Someone had dumped it into trash cans behind a foundry."

"Such a waste."

"A funny thing. The dogs and raccoons might have done it, but there is a stronger possibility that whoever dumped that meat unwrapped it first."

19

MARGE had gone off without so much as a by-your-leave and Anthony Mendax was, in his own words, mightily pissed off. This was simply no way to run a railroad. He had been on the citizen band to the office without result, and when he parked behind his building he entered by an unlocked door to find an empty suite of offices, no Marge anywhere, not even a note indicating where the hell she had gone. He dialed her home and sat grinding his teeth while the bell rang and rang unanswered. He slammed the phone down and lit a cigarette.

Against his better judgment, he had read his horoscope that morning in the Kenosha *Times*. Proceed with caution in business opportunities; success will come as a surprise, not an achievement. Mendax snorted. His disdain was the more profound because he had once been more influenced by those ridiculous one-liners on his daily destiny than he would have cared to admit. And then he had met the prick who wrote them, a cynical lush who tapped them out with no concern for the fact that more people than you would believe guide their day by the nonsense he wrote.

"Serves the bastards right," Bacon said, showing yellowed teeth. "Superstition."

Was it possible that, no matter what Bacon thought he was doing, the powers-that-be used him? Bacon had come up with some uncanny advice in the past, there was no denying it. Luck, of course. Coincidence. Mendax folded the *Times* and threw it on the floor. You read that sort of garbage and are influenced by it, you make it come true. Still, he wondered what Bacon had had to say to Libras on Tuesday. He had half a mind to check up on it. He would not be surprised to find that he had been warned against traveling south.

Had he not had, on the drive down, an intimation that this was not his bag at all? What he was attempting to do certainly meant treading a fine line from a legal point of view. Still and all, if he had found the old doll home and asked her to make out her check to Anima Mundi Publications, who could prove it was fraud? The point was academic now, of course. But Anthony Mendax did not like being made to look a fool, and when he had driven away from that house, with that silly old priest seeing him on his way, he felt like the victim of a very unfunny practical joke. It was a possibility he had still not discarded. That priest—what was his name, Dowling?—was probably no more of a priest than Mendax himself. Never con a con? Don't you believe it.

Mendax lay back in his executive chair, puffing on his cigarette, glowering at the ceiling. It was a vexing thought that he had dozens of enemies who could have pulled such a stunt, watched him fall for the bait and died laughing. Maybe Dowling had got the whole damned thing on tape because of course no joke could be complete until Mendax knew they knew. But no. He could not believe it. It was too elaborate a setup for a couple of laughs. And even if Sylvia Lowry had not been there, she did exist. So what was going on?

He did not really need to feel victimized by enemies. Fate, the fickle finger thereof, was villain enough. There was a Sylvia Lowry and if he had hit her under optimum circumstances he would have had fifty thou in the kitty, no strings attached. She wanted Masses? He would have arranged for Masses, and he would have struck a better bargain than she had been willing to accept.

Even now, thinking of that money, his mouth watered. It would have been the answer to everything. He had always been stymied by lack of capital. Why, he could have quadrupled that fifty grand before you could say Sylvia Lowry. Any number of ideas he had had to put in escrow for lack of money could have been put in play. He meant the sign on his lawn, the legend on his stationery: it was Anthony Mendax Enterprises, Inc. Enterprises, plural; he had dreamed of becoming the Renaissance man of the business world, a one-man conglomerate, idea man, financier, administrator, salesman, everything in one.

A glance around his office brought home to him the distance between where he was and what he had dreamed of. Where in the hell was Marge? Fire the bitch. Ha. She knew too much; she was too reliable; she was, he remembered, an officer of at least two of his corporations, largely paper affairs, but honest to God. Nothing like a title to offer in lieu of money, though he had thought Marge had a better head on her shoulders. She was treasurer of one, vice-president of another Mendax company, and she must derive some solace from those titles when she considered her inadequate paycheck.

There was the sound of a car passing up the drive and coming to a stop in back.

Mendax checked and saw that it was Marge and was back in his chair rocking nonchalantly, though with a frown that could not be ignored, when she came in.

"You're here," she said, collapsing into a chair across the room from him. Her arms hung limp and her shoes began to slide out from the chair. She aged before his eyes.

"Yes, I am here. Of course, it might have been anyone. I see your point. The door was wide open. Come in, one and all, give me your tired, your poor, use my office, rifle my desk . . ."

He stopped. He was being ignored. Marge was staring at the floor and her eyes had filmed over with tears. Mendax, welcoming a new role, sprang to his feet.

"Marge, Marge, what is it? What's wrong?"

She sobbed. "Why didn't they just go ahead and exhume the body, for God's sake, it couldn't have hit her harder. Bring it all back, throw it in her face, and just when finally, after two years, she was getting over it, not feeling guilty about being alive."

"What body? Marge, who did this?"

"The police."

"Dug up a body? Okay. Whose body? What has this to do with you? You've got no buried bodies, Marge."

"My sister!" She looked at him as if he had just flunked a very elementary test in *Reader's Digest:* test your boss, grade him yourself, do you work for an idiot?

"Your sister's body?"

"Her husband. You knew him, Tony. He stood in this room and talked to you. A wonderful man."

Tony stepped backward, his hands opening in a sacerdotal gesture. It was beginning to take shape for him. Marge's brother-in-law. Small-time contractor. He had been in on the renovation of this house. Bit of a quarrel then over the bill. So he had been appointed officer of one of the . . . Anima Mundi! That was it. He was the treasurer of Anima Mundi. Owen Bartley. Mendax moved back behind his desk.

Was there no coincidence left in the whole goddam world? Did everything conspire? He poured them both a cup of coffee, gave Marge hers, got back behind his desk.

"Tell me all about it, Marge. From the beginning. Your sister called you here at the office?"

Called her in hysterics, the police were at the house asking questions about Owen as if the man were still among the living and not two years dead. Carlotta wanted Marge to get right over there before she had a nervous breakdown or worse. Marge of course had gone, just ran right out to her car —Mendax dismissed this, closed his eyes, shook his head, it was nothing, it did not matter—and honest to God there was a patrol car parked in front of her sister's house, bold as brass. What would the neighbors think? What would they say? Carlotta had locked her lips and thrown away the key.

"So I asked the police what it was all about. I took one of them aside and said for the love of God Owen died two years ago and you come in here asking questions of his widow. He wanted the date of death. How would I know the date of death? I asked Carlotta and she began to wail. It's the funeral all over again. Finally we get the date of Owen's death out of her. The cop writes it down."

"Did he say why he was interested in Owen?"

"Just routine. He kept saying that. Just routine."

"You had a right to know. You shouldn't have told him a thing."

"I wish you had been there, Tony. I told Carlotta the same thing. What could I tell them? Nothing. The date of Owen's death."

"What else did they want to know?"

"Where he worked."

"They would know all that. Weren't they locals?"

"Kenosha Keystone Regulars. But it's not a local

matter, this young punk says. He has a tablet and he keeps scribbling in it. Big deal."

"Not a local matter."

"He didn't know what it was."

This seemed one more shade of gloom to add to the cloud that had been hanging over his head since that dumdum trip to Illinois. He should go into seclusion until his stars got into a more favorable conjunction. Libra. He had thought it meant free; the scales a symbol of a free weigh-in.

"The questions they asked, Tony. What had Carlotta done with her husband's effects. His effects! Until a few months ago she had them draped around that house so it looked like a shrine to Owen Bartley."

"What kind of effects?"

"His check book. His identification. His credit cards."

20

McGINNIS, his white hair like cotton wadding above a red face meant to be merry but forever wearing an expression of professional commiseration, beckoned Father Dowling away from the viewing room and down the hall to his office. Inside, he suggested a drink, perhaps knowing Dowling must refuse.

"I wanted a word with you before you saw the body,

Father," McGinnis joined his fat little hands and shook his head as if in tune with the sorrow of the world. "I hate to think what August Lowry would say if he saw her laid out in that pitiful box."

"He would say what anyone does who comes here, Harry. You do a remarkable job at the McGinnis Funeral Home."

"Thank you, Father. I know you mean it and that makes it the more welcome. We do what we can, whatever the wishes of the bereaved, and I think I can say no one has gone away from here with the idea that he did not have the wherewithal for a worthy and honorable funeral for his loved one."

"I'm sure of that."

"But, Father, when they can have more than the minimum, when it is not a question of pinching pennies, when it is a lady like Sylvia Lowry, well, that is another matter."

"I believe James Lowry made the arrangements?"

McGinnis wore a distasteful expression. "A wretched man. He was a promising boy. He still is, I suspect. The clothes on the man. A fop, that's what he is. A dude. And the man actually has the education of a dentist."

"So I'm told." Dowling stole a glance at his watch. It was still fifteen minutes before the scheduled rosary, and he was willing to waste a few more minutes here with McGinnis.

Apparently Jimmy Lowry had taken to heart the warning that McGinnis would have been delighted to lower ten thousand dollars of Lowry money into Sylvia's grave if he could persuade the family to part with it. If McGinnis could be believed, Jimmy had sinned in the opposite direction. He had not insisted on the legendary plain pine box, but he had been adamant about keeping to the least expensive range of coffins. McGinnis's point seemed to be that, however sturdy these were, worth every penny, he wasn't suggesting otherwise, nonetheless, and he tried to make the point both delicately and clearly to Dr. Lowry, they simply were not waterproof.

"Well, it's too late now."

"I suppose. I suppose. I just wanted you to understand."

"And I do. I'm glad you mentioned it to me."

"I don't imagine it would do any good for you to say something . . ."

"No," Dowling said firmly. "I am sure it would not. I am really not close to the family."

"Poor Sylvia Lowry," McGinnis said, abruptly changing keys. He seemed genuinely, as opposed to professionally, sad.

"Yes."

"A dreadful way to go."

"Do you think it was painful?"

"Oh my, I hope not. Not that you'll be able to tell she met a violent end. She looks like an angel, Father. An angel."

And so she did, an aged angel, lying in what looked to be a very nice coffin indeed, her hair done but not overdone, her fine features outlined against the plush opened top of the coffin. A pale blue dress, her rosary beads entwined in her hands. Father Dowling saw that they were not the ones Sylvia had actually used, those that had hung at her bedpost. He mentioned this to Jimmy Lowry, who was dressed in a navy blue blazer and subdued slacks.

"McGinnis supplied the rosary. Does it matter?"

"No. Of course not."

"They all look alike."

"More or less."

The Cordwills stood a few feet away and Father Dowling went to them. Sharon's face was puffy. She wore black. She seemed still drugged. Had she really taken her mother's death so hard? Cheryl was already seated in a front row. There was a woman Father Dowling did not know on the other side of Bill Cordwill.

"Have you met Harriet, Father?"

"No, I haven't."

"Harriet Firth." She gave him her gloved hand. "I was always so fond of Sylvia."

Jimmy had not come along when Dowling moved to say hello to the Cordwills and it might have been the presence of his wife, his ex-wife, that explained this. Was Harriet Firth welcome here or not? It was difficult to discern the Cordwills' reaction. Bill might have been a mortician himself, his manner and bearing had adjusted so remarkably to these circumstances. He guided Sharon to a chair beside their daughter. Harriet sat on the other side of her niece. Jimmy hovered.

The other rows were full of friends, friends and the curious. Dowling recognized many faces from the pews of St. Hilary's, among them Edna Hospers and her husband. Dowling finally caught the attention of those still chatting at the back of the room, there were a few shushes, and then silence fell. He announced that they would now recite the rosary for the repose of the soul of Sylvia Lowry.

He knelt on the *prie-dieu* in front of the casket, his back to the room, and began the Apostles' Creed. Soon the rhythm of praying priest and answering congregation was established, Dowling saying the beginning of an Our Father, the people completing it, and then a decade of Hail Marys, five decades in all, the Sorrowful Mysteries.

The origin of the rosary is in one way clear, in another shrouded in the mystery of tradition. In the form it is now said by Catholics, it goes back to the thirteenth century, to Dominic, the founder of the Order of Preachers, the Dominicans. The rosary is the prayer Our Lady urged upon Dominic and his new order of mendicant friars in their struggle against the Albigensians. It has waxed and waned in favor among the faithful, but has never fallen into complete neglect—not even today, when it has been the object of much thoughtless criticism by liturgical enthusiasts and ecumenical cheerleaders.

Dowling could remember fifteen or twenty years before, when the saying of the rosary at Mass, instead of reading the missal, had been frowned upon. Now anything like private devotion was being attacked in the liturgical razzle-dazzle that had gained such momentum under the ill-fated Vatican II. There were times when Dowling doubted that anyone at all still said the rosary, but then a wake revived his faith that it persisted as a regular element of the prayer life of many. Somehow on such occasions rosaries were produced, and it seemed safe to assume they were sometimes said in more joyful moments.

As it had before, the recurrent plea, pray for us now and at the hour of our death, seemed to have a special pertinence to Sylvia Lowry. He hoped her prayer had indeed been answered during the dreadful events of last Monday. But his prayer also included her slayer. Keegan had to see all this as a case to be solved, but there was a soul, perhaps several souls, in grievous danger, and that must be the concern of a priest and the object of his prayers. He asked God that he or she or they would see the horror of what they had done and beg His forgiveness. Little matter then if they were apprehended and punished by the civil law, so long as they had confessed their guilt to God and received His pardon. They were not, after all, so different from the rest of men, for who does not need God's pardon, who is without sin?

Of course, it would not do to take this tack with Keegan. The man had a job to do and Dowling wished him well in it. It was simply that their tasks were different.

"William Cordwill?" Keegan had said when they were talking of what members of the family had been doing last Monday. The detective shook his head. "It's the same thing, Roger. We know what he was doing but it still leaves the possibility open."

"I suppose he was at work."

"He had gone to Chicago on business."

"I see."

"He had an appointment and he kept it. But there is no way of being certain he left Fox River when he said he did or that he returned when he said he did. A little spare time at either end would have been sufficient."

"So it comes down to Monday and Tuesday."

"It does indeed."

"And what have you found out about those days?"

Keegan could not keep the pleased look from his face and Father Dowling felt a sinking sensation in his stomach. He did not want it to be any of the family. It would be so much more convenient to have suspicion turn to a stranger—the alleged Father Winter from Dubuque, for instance. But of course if it did and he came to know Winter better, he would feel the same anguish at the thought of a man falling into the machinery of the state. Too often such a fate hardened the heart and fostered a false sense of injustice so that true sorrow came harder, if at all. The criminal has learned to blame society and not himself, which is why Father Dowling preferred the sinner to the criminal—even when they were the same person.

"They were all at the house during those two days."

"All of them?"

"Not together, you understand. But each one of them made at least one trip to the house during the time their mother was supposedly a missing person and flown off from O'Hare airport."

With an effort Roger Dowling shrugged away these distractions and concentrated on the prayers and mysteries of the lives of Our Lord and Our Lady, which one was supposed to meditate on while murmuring the repetitive prayers. "The Fifth Sorrowful Mystery," he intoned. "The crucifixion of Our Lord and Savior Jesus Christ."

When they were done, the routine that had preceded the saying of the rosary re-established itself. People formed small groups, exchanging gossip, and from time to time someone would come forward to express his condolences to one of the family and then kneel for a moment before the open coffin on the *prie-dieu* Father Dowling had used, to say a prayer for Sylvia. A distracted prayer, of course, since there is nothing like the sight of a corpse, even one prepared for viewing by the redoubtable McGinnis, to turn one's mind inward to thoughts of one's own mortality. The mourners prayed for Sylvia and felt, if only briefly, sorry for themselves. And of course it was *de rigueur* to sign the Visitors Book, lest it go unrecorded that this sad duty to the departed had been fulfilled.

Dowling noticed that Cheryl still kept aloof, still sat alone on her chair in the first row. Something in the disapproving way the child was observing the behavior of the adults drew Dowling to the chair beside her.

"Would you like to go outside for a breath of fresh air?"

She looked at him. "Would it be okay?"

"Come on."

They went out the door that opened off the hallway leading to McGinnis's office, an exit that enabled them to avoid pushing through the crowd. They came out onto the far end of the parking lot into a cool night. A quarter moon was sliding through thin trailing clouds. All around them rose the racket of crickets.

"Isn't this better, Cheryl?"

She nodded. They began to walk up and down on the asphalt. Cheryl retained her silence.

"Death is a mystery," Dowling said helplessly. As soon as he said the silly words, he wished he could take them back. "Your grandmother is at peace now."

"When will they catch the man who killed her?"

"You mustn't worry about that."

"Do you think they will?"

"Are you frightened? Don't be. It is the person who killed your grandmother who is frightened now. Can you imagine what it must be like to carry a burden like that on your soul? Let us hope God catches him. I don't mean to punish him. To save him. That is what your grandmother would want."

"But what if it isn't like that? What if he isn't frightened at all?"

"I'm sure he is."

"If I know who did it, shouldn't I tell the police?"

"Do you know who did it?"

They turned to walk back to the dark part of the lot from which they had come.

"Yes."

"I suppose you could send the police a note."

She started to speak, but stopped herself.

"You wouldn't have to let them know who sent it. You could clip the words from a newspaper."

Cheryl stopped walking. "I already did."

"I know."

"Who told you?"

"They didn't tell me it was you who sent the note. Why do you think it was your Uncle Jimmy?"

"He broke Grandma's heart. Ask Mama and Daddy. He didn't care for her at all. He stopped being a dentist and divorced his wife and began to make a lot of money and act silly."

"That may be, but why do you think he killed your grandmother?"

"Daddy thinks so too."

"Did he ask you to send the note?"

"Oh no. He doesn't know about it. I don't want him to know."

"But he thinks your Uncle Jimmy killed your grandma?"

Cheryl nodded.

"Did he say that?"

Cheryl looked shrewd. "I knew what he meant. The other day we did some errands together, and we were talking about Grandma."

"Before she was found?"

"This was on Tuesday. We stopped at the cleaners with some things."

"Did your father think your grandmother was dead then?"

She seemed surprised and a little confused. Dowling did not want to increase her confusion. He took her hand and they went back the length of the parking lot, into the brightly lighted area where most of the cars were parked. From the open doors of the funeral home came the sound of those inside, their voices emerging into the great vault of the night echoing with crickets. It might have been a party.

21

THE KENOSHA police had been efficient as well as cooperative. So had the State Patrol. Anthony Mendax was furious when he was brought into Keegan's office.

"Please sit down, Mr. Mendax."

"Sit down! I've been sitting on my tochus for hours while I was being shanghaied. What the hell is this all about?"

"You have a right to counsel, Mr. Mendax. You are under no obligation to say anything."

"Obligation! Try and stop me. I don't need a lawyer. I've done nothing wrong."

Keegan sighed. "You rented a car using the credit card of a man who is dead."

"Owen Bartley. He was an associate of mine."

"And you signed his name."

"I was in a hurry. I gave the girl the wrong card and rather than go through the whole rigmarole again I signed Bartley's name. Is that a federal offense?"

"It may be, yes. But that is not our interest."

"You dragged me across a state line to talk about a credit card?"

Mendax made it sound as if Keegan were in violation of the Mann Act.

"You paid a visit in this city dressed as a priest."

Mendax sat down. He looked almost relieved. "Does this town have a dress code? Come on, you didn't bring me all this way for wearing a clerical collar."

"No denial then?"

"What's to deny? I rented a car with an old friend's credit card—by mistake—and I have eccentric tastes in clothes." Mendax sat forward. "When I talk to a lawyer, Sergeant . . ."

"Captain."

"Captain, Colonel, Field Marshal. When I talk to a lawyer it will be about false arrest, harassment, and whatever else he dreams up."

"You told the Kenosha police you had received a letter from Mrs. Sylvia Lowry asking you to come see her."

"That's right."

"Could you tell me why?"

"It's a business matter, Captain. If the lady doesn't want to reveal the reason, I don't feel free to either."

"You're referring to Sylvia Lowry?"

"Is there another lady involved?"

"Sylvia Lowry is dead, Mr. Mendax."

The feisty look left Mendax's jowly face, leaving only gray flesh.

"She was murdered."

"Oh my God. Look, as God is my judge, I never even met the woman. She wasn't home when I went there. A priest answered the door."

"We know about that."

"When did she—die?"

"She was murdered on Monday, shortly after noon."

"Monday!" The color came back into Mendax's face. "Monday at noon? I was here on Tuesday. On Monday I was in Kenosha."

"Is this the letter you received from Mrs. Lowry?" Keegan held out a pink page to Mendax.

"Where did you get that?"

"From your office. With a warrant. This is an investigation of murder, Mr. Mendax."

"But if she was killed on Monday . . ."

"The Kenosha police cannot account for your whereabouts on Monday. You were not in your office."

"Of course I wasn't in my office. I was making calls."

"On whom?"

Mendax stared at Keegan. He pulled a small book from the inside pocket of his orange sports jacket, flipped it open, and consulted it. He looked like a boy who had not prepared his lesson. The man's secretary had told the Kenosha police Mendax had had no appointments on Monday.

Keegan continued. "Mrs. Lowry wrote you offering to donate fifty thousand dollars to your religious work. Let me get this straight. Are you a priest?"

"I am not a priest."

"Are you a minister?"

Mendax shook his head.

"Do you make any claim whatsoever to being a man of religion?"

"That is a rather broad description," Mendax said, but his heart was not in the words. His mind still seemed to be groping through memories of Monday, desperate for an alibi.

"Admittedly. Have you ever claimed to be a minister or a priest?"

"No."

"Yet Mrs. Lowry wrote you under the assumption that you are a priest. What is Anima Mundi?"

"It is a corporation of which I am president. We publish booklets, tracts, religious pamphlets. Mrs. Lowry refers to one of our publications in her letter. It was on the assumption that she wished to contribute to the work of Anima Mundi that I came to see her. Unsuccessfully, I must add. I never saw the woman. Never."

"You came wearing a Roman collar?"

"And met someone else wearing one. Look, find that other priest. That priest." Mendax stopped. "If he is a priest."

"He is a priest."

"You've found him?"

Keegan nodded.

"Then he must have told you I didn't even meet the Lowry woman. I wasn't in the house ten minutes. I drove back to O'Hare, turned in the car, and drove my own back to Kenosha."

"We know you didn't see Mrs. Lowry on Tuesday."

Mendax beamed. "That's what I said."

"She was already dead. I believe I mentioned she was killed on Monday."

"Well, I'm sorry to hear that. But on Monday I was nowhere near Fox River, Illinois."

"But you won't tell me where you were."

"What is this? Do I have to prove I'm innocent? For God's sake, this is America. I am innocent. I don't have to prove it."

"Mr. Mendax, Mrs. Sylvia Lowry was killed sometime after noon on Monday. The Kenosha police cannot account for your whereabouts from ten o'clock Monday morning until you rented the car at O'Hare on Tuesday. From Monday until early on Wednesday, we thought Mrs. Lowry was a missing person. Her car had been left at O'Hare airport. But all that time her body was in a freezer chest in her basement."

"Come on."

"In a freezer chest. Put there by the killer in order to gain time. He wanted attention directed away from that house.

We know Mrs. Lowry had a large amount of money in her house. You were promised money by her, however mistakenly on her part. Did she suspect her mistake on Monday? Did you strike her and then, perhaps in a panic, want to get rid of the body? Or did you coolly decide that now you could make a thorough search of the house? So you put her body in the freezer . . ."

Mendax was shaking his head in disbelief, but his smile was forced.

"On Monday your search was interrupted several times and on Tuesday when you returned, Father Dowling answered the door. Scared off by this, you returned to Kenosha without your fifty thousand dollars."

"It's true that a priest opened the door when I went to the house on Tuesday. It is also true that I returned to Kenosha without any fifty thousand dollars. As for the rest of it, Captain, it is pure malarkey."

"Not pure malarkey. Speculative, yes."

Keegan was reluctant to book Mendax on what he had, though what he had made an interesting picture. Mendax was pretty much what he had expected, the entrepreneur devolved into confidence man. Hogan, the city prosecutor, was about as helpful as Morton the coroner. Hogan wobbled his hand back and forth when Keegan had asked him if they had enough to hold Mendax. "It's touch and go, Captain."

"I need an arrest."

Hogan understood. The editorial in the evening paper had been a jeremiad on crime in the streets, on unsolved crimes, and had taken Sylvia Lowry's murder as proof that citizens were no longer safe in the privacy of their own homes. Something had to be done, the anonymous editorialist had thundered. Something had to be done, and not next year or next month or next week. Fox River could demand no less.

"Do you think he did it, Phil?"

Keegan wobbled his own hand. "It's not impossible."

"I think you can proceed."

There was backing for you. Keegan did not like the idea of proceeding against Mendax just to satisfy the newspaper that was and had been the fiefdom of the Hapsgood family for three generations, the Hapsgoods who had embraced with unction the apologia of Gardner Cowles for the one-newspaper town. Without vulgar competition, the argument ran, the public was better served with an objective diet of news. How the hell could the public ever know that was true? Keegan found this an odd conception of freedom of the press. But then, freedom of the press is an odd conception. Anyone with a few million dollars at his disposal could start a newspaper in a town the size of Fox River. As for Chicago, New York, Washington, a major city, the ante was astronomical, not to mention the fact that there vulgar competition might jeopardize your investment. Keegan had no desire at all to placate Hapsgood. What he did want to do was to lull the killer into thinking suspicion was pointed elsewhere. And for this purpose Anthony Mendax of Kenosha, Wisconsin, was a gift of the gods. And of course Mendax could have killed Mrs. Lowry. Keegan had not been without hope that something new might have emerged from this interview.

"How often have you used Owen Bartley's credit card?"

The question rattled Mendax, Keegan did not understand why.

"Frequently?"

"No, of course not."

"Just recently?"

Mendax seemed to coil in his chair. "Goddam it, are you charging me with something or not?"

"Yes."

Like most decisions, it was made without being made. Some instinct told Keegan that the clue to breaking Mendax lay in that credit card. He rang for Lieutenant Horvath and instructed him to take Mendax out and book him on suspicion of murder.

"Murder! Jesus Christ." Mendax lifted from the chair as if a spring had released beneath him. "No! I swear to God I never even met the woman. You can't do this to me. I am a businessman."

"I suggest you engage counsel immediately." Keegan looked at Horvath. "He can use the phone all he wants."

Mendax left the room slowly, reluctantly, incredulously. He kept looking at Keegan as if he expected this farce to be stopped. Keegan was unimpressed. No two guilty people acted alike when accused. No one in his heart of hearts seemed to believe himself really guilty of anything. Or is it that we believe that anything we have done can be undone? It is rather difficult to undo a murder.

Keegan stood and stretched. For the first time he almost believed Anthony Mendax had killed Sylvia Lowry. And would it not be best all around if he had?

22

BILL CORDWILL pulled into the drive-in window of Merlin's Cleaners and waited for the gum-chewing girl to open the window and push the receiving counter out to where it almost touched the car. He put a ticket on the counter.

"I want these things. Even if they're not done," he called as the girl wheeled from the window and disappeared among the plastic bags hanging on racks. Her face emerged with a quizzical look. She studied the slip.

"They won't be done. You didn't say it was a rush."

"Okay. It doesn't matter. Just give them back."

"A suit, right?"

"That's right."

"It's not back yet. It was picked up on Wednesday."

"Picked up?"

"Taken to the factory. We don't do the cleaning here."

Of course they didn't. He should have known that. He got the address of the cleaning plant and drove away. He was perspiring more than the temperature accounted for, though it was a hot day. Cheryl's account of her conversation with Father Dowling had put his mind in gear. How in the world had she inferred from anything he had said that Jimmy had killed Sylvia? Bill was certain he had not said that. It was unnerving to think what a kid got out of anything you said. Had she noticed his reaction when she reminded him of their conversation on the way to the dry cleaners? He did not dare ask her if she had mentioned that errand to Dowling. Better to assume she had and take every precaution, no matter how far-fetched.

The factory did not look like a place where clothes went to become clean. It was a dirty old building that had seen other uses than its present one. Doors were open everywhere, and no wonder. The heat inside, added to the temperature of the July day, was excruciating. The manager worked in a small cube of an office set in one corner of the huge floor, no windows, but an air conditioner driven through an outside wall that tugged, with much rattling and wheezing, moisture from the air. Bill Cordwill laid his ticket on the manager's desk.

"I want to pick up this suit."

The man was in white: white shirt, white pants. His black belt, threaded through the white loops of the trousers, seemed to emit a monotonous code. Dash, dash, dash. The manager stared at the slip as if he had never seen its like before.

"From Merlin's."

The factory cleaned clothes for any number of smaller firms—so much for the advertised claims of differentiated service.

"That's right."

"You from the police?"

"Good Lord, no."

The man looked up with milky eyes.

"Your name Cordwill?"

"Why would you think I'm from the police?"

"Because they already picked up your suit."

He stared into the unfathomable expression in the manager's eyes. Did his own expression change? He thought not. Indeed, he surprised himself with his calmness. He nodded as if an esoteric theory had just been verified.

"Good," he said.

"You want your suit, you got to talk to the police."

Bill nodded. Of course. This happened all the time.

"They had a warrant. They had a right."

Bill left the office, closing the door behind him. Would the manager now call the police? Anything was possible. He had not seriously thought he was in any danger because of the suit; he had thought he was merely being careful. In his car, he started the motor and thought of the plan that had brought him here. Pick up the suit and get rid of it. He realized now it had not been clear how he was going to accomplish this. Suddenly the suit seemed as large as this cleaning factory—impossible to ignore, impossible to hide. Through the open doors he could see the workers, all in white, tending to their hellish tasks. The door of the office opened and the manager appeared. Despite all the distractions and obstacles between them, his eyes seemed to go directly to Bill Cordwill sitting in his car.

Bill put the car in reverse, made a U turn in the lot, and drove away, not swiftly, just drove away. What in the name of God was he going to do now?

23

WHEN Father Dowling came downstairs he was stopped by the sound of a voice in the kitchen. He gripped the knob of the newel post and tried not to make the identification, but it was impossible not to. He shook his head as if to empty it and turned, meaning to flee upstairs to his room, but the stair beneath him creaked and there was silence in the kitchen.

"Is that you, Father Dowling?"

He stopped. He might have been playing a game. Simon says.

"Father Dowling?"

Marie Murkin stood in the kitchen door. Alone. She looked at him curiously while he sought an indifferent expression.

"Yes?"

"I almost forgot. It's time for the funeral, isn't it?"

Dowling nodded, willing that the other should stay out of sight, remain in the kitchen, not put him in the position of having a face to match the voice that had whispered so urgently to him through the grille of the confessional. But his will was inefficacious.

"Hi, Father."

"Gene is here to take a look at my television. He said you asked him to."

Dowling nodded. He could not by manner or expression convey to Gene Hospers that he connected him with the penitent in the confessional box.

"You might take a look at the one in the study too."

"What's wrong with it, Father?"

"The picture is very weak when I watch NBC."

"That's common around here. Don't know quite why it is."

"Take a look at it, will you?"

Hospers gave him a jaunty little salute by way of reply and Dowling went out the side door and along the walk to the sacristy. Another hot day, sun relentless, a cloudless sky and the birds singing their hearts out. It seemed incongruous weather for a funeral, except to a liturgist perhaps. The funeral Mass now put the emphasis on resurrection, joy, and hope. Dowling considered this psychologically if not theologically wrong. It tended to suggest that death was of small moment and grief an aberration. Yet Our Lord had wept over Lazarus and He had feared to die Himself. Those proofs of Christ's humanity seemed put in question by a liturgy that called for smiles and false bravura. Couldn't people be permitted the comfort of their tears, the somberness of black, the triste rhythm of the *Dies Irae?*

Ten minutes later he was standing vested at the front door of the church to meet the hearse. McGinnis and his assistant bustled about. The pallbearers did what they were told. They were old, Sylvia's vintage, friends of her husband, survivors. The family got out of the two following cars, looking sober enough. They might have been electric charges held together by offsetting forces of repulsion. William Cordwill was white as a sheet, Jimmy nervous, Sharon apparently still under sedation. The arrest of Anthony Mendax had provided no discernible consolation to the victim's family.

"Do you really think he did it?" Dowling had asked Keegan on the phone.

"Don't you?"

"I have no idea," Dowling said evenly.

"The widow of the man whose credit card he used has brought charges against him in Kenosha. She claims he must have stolen the card. Mendax had several other documents of Owen Bartley's."

"Of course he is a charlatan. But you have arrested him for murder."

"On suspicion of second-degree homicide, to be exact."

"I don't suppose he was obliging enough to have a great deal of unaccounted-for cash among his stolen credit cards?"

"Someone must have gotten that money."

"Someone? If it wasn't Mendax, how can you hold him?"

"Getting the money isn't conclusive. How frequently do you suppose murderers fail to gain the objective they murder for?"

"The money is gone."

Keegan made a corrective noise. "We don't know that."

"Think, Phil."

"Tell me what I should think about, Roger."

"About Sylvia Lowry's temporary tomb."

"I'll do that," Keegan had said. The conversation ended on a less than cordial note and Dowling regretted having suggested to Phil what he had doubtless already seen.

Having sprinkled the coffin with holy water, Dowling stood aside so the pallbearers could precede him down the aisle with their burden. The family, under the sibilant urging of McGinnis, fell in behind the priest.

As he had been at the funeral home, Father Dowling was half surprised by the turnout. Sylvia had been such a lonely little creature, it was easy to forget that her husband had been a very prominent man who was still remembered. Of course there were the parish regulars, people who made a habit of attending funerals and weddings. Like the priest, these veteran spectators must have categories into which to fit types of mourners. Sylvia's family would no doubt be classified as a cool bunch, going numbly through the motions, clearly anxious to have this over and done with.

Even later, at the cemetery, there was no display of emotion. Sharon seemed to sag against her husband and Jimmy grew more pensive when the casket was lifted to the lowering contraption above the open grave and Dowling began to read the final obsequies. A canopy had been placed over the gravesite, and though it was a windless day there was the sound of snapping canvas competing with Dowling as he read. And then it was over. Dowling received perfunctory handshakes from Jimmy and Bill and there were the first awkward movements toward the waiting cars.

"God rest her soul," McGinnis said cheerfully when Dowling got in beside him.

"Amen."

"August Lowry was wise to buy that lot when he did. It won't be long before we bury the last body in that cemetery."

"Then what?"

"Out of town. Or . . ." McGinnis sneaked a look at Dowling. "Where do you stand on cremation, Father?"

"It will come."

"It's got to, Father. It's got to."

The Church's ban on cremation had been a defensive

tactic, a response to Masonic attack. It was all history now. Cremation could be as respectful a way to treat the body as burial, just so long as the body was treated for what it had been, the temple of the Holy Ghost.

McGinnis was not concerned with history. "It's a lot more sanitary, Father. If the truth were known."

"You meant the meat," Keegan said. They were seated in the rectory study, the Cubs game on the set.

"Yes."

"He cleaned it out to make room for the body."

Dowling affected to be interested in a missed double play. He did not even want to think of what he knew and Keegan could not. The seal of the confessional bound, to the degree this is possible, even the confessor's private thoughts. But the television set was there to prompt the unwanted associations and, almost angrily, Dowling struck a match and held it to his pipe. His pipe was already lit and drawing well.

"So your guess is that the money was in the freezer too?"

Dowling shrugged. Keegan had a habit of attributing his own theories to Dowling. "You said there was a new development."

"Mendax is out on bail."

"I'm not surprised."

"His lawyer agreed to keep him in town. If only to avoid running into other charges in Kenosha."

Dowling smiled. He would like to see Mendax again. Would it cheer the man up to be told he had made a rather convincing priest? Keegan had lifted his beer glass and seemed to be consulting it as if it were an oracle.

"What is it, Phil?"

"You may remember telling me of your conversation with the Cordwill girl."

"With Cheryl? Yes, I remember."

"Something you said caught my attention."

"I knew it would."

"The errand they went on."

"Then you checked the dry cleaners, Phil?"

Keegan's head jerked and he glared at Dowling. "How the devil?" He shook his head in disgust. "Yes, we checked the dry cleaners."

"And?"

"A suit. There was a stain on the left shoulder. A bloodstain."

"Sylvia's blood?"

"Yes."

"Dear God. What will you do now?"

"I thought you might wish to advise me, Father Dowling," Phil said half sarcastically.

"I wouldn't presume to do that, Captain Keegan."

"Like fun you wouldn't."

"You haven't done anything yet?"

"I've asked Cordwill to come in tomorrow morning. Of course we're keeping an eye on him. If he does something foolish, it will make things easier in the morning. I almost wish it had been Anthony Mendax."

"Don't rule him out."

"Look, Roger, I know you enjoy playing detective. Everybody does. I enjoy it myself, for crying out loud. But think. Blood on his suit and just where you'd expect to find it if he carried the body downstairs."

"I know."

"Well, then."

"But who carried it upstairs again?"

"If I can prove he carried it down . . ."

"I'm sure you can. But when was the suit taken to the cleaners? On Tuesday? The body was still in the freezer then, was it not? The suit won't help you show that Bill Cordwill carried the body upstairs again."

"Do you seriously think that, if he put her into the freezer, it was someone else who took her out?"

"It seems more plausible than that he would. I am sure he has a lot to answer for, but I doubt that he carried the body upstairs again."

Keegan chose to ignore this doubt in favor of what seemed certainties.

"He put her body into the freezer after he had emptied it of its contents."

"Well, after it had been emptied of its contents, anyway. But by him? We don't know. And isn't it true that you would have to prove he took the meat to where you found it? That ought to be easily enough done. I don't suppose you could haul all that frozen meat around in a car during a July heat wave without leaving traces."

"I'm going to get another beer."

Through the murmur of the televised ball game Dowling heard Keegan using the kitchen telephone. The priest felt he had just done Bill Cordwill a service.

"I'll tell you one thing," Keegan said when he was once again in his chair. He had remembered to bring a fresh bottle of beer with him from the kitchen. "Whoever did haul that meat around killed Sylvia Lowry."

"That should come as a great relief to your man Mendax."

"My man!" Keegan snorted.

"That would leave only one missing link."

Keegan did not answer, but his tension did not seem explained by the foredoomed game. Jack Brickhouse talked on, whistling in the dark, loyal beyond the limits of rationality.

"You will have to find the person who carried the body up from the basement."

24

BEFORE he had Bill Cordwill admitted to his office, Keegan gave Horvath explicit instructions.

"After you bring in Cordwill," he concluded.

"His wife is with him."

"Well, I don't want her in here."

"He's clinging to her as if his life depended on her."

Keegan did not like that. A man should stand up and answer for his deeds. There was no need to drag his wife through this, no matter how willing she might be.

"Just Cordwill," he said to Horvath.

But when the door opened a moment later it was Sharon Cordwill who entered.

"The lieutenant said you wanted me to wait outside while you talk to Bill." She said it as if with disbelief and a little half smile flitted across her face.

"I want to ask your husband some questions."

"Of course you do. We understand that. We are eager to tell you everything you wish to know." She had come directly to his desk and now the tips of her fingers pressed against its surface. Her voice dropped. "My husband is extremely overwrought, Captain Keegan. I think it is advisable that I be with him during this ordeal."

"Mrs. Cordwill, I assure you . . ."

"I insist on it," she said evenly. "We have not brought counsel. We could delay this appointment by arranging for counsel. Would you care to have to discuss with a lawyer my right to be with my husband?"

Keegan did not take defeat gracefully, though he had to admit, not at the time but later, that Sharon Cordwill made it easy for him. When she saw she had won, she congratulated Keegan for his understanding.

"I'll tell Bill you want to question us now."

A sleepless night had not been beneficial to Bill Cordwill's appearance. His eyes were sunken and shot with blood. Only the beautifully tailored suit, gray with dark blue tie, and his usual grooming saved him. His wife got him settled in one chair before Keegan's desk and then she herself sat in its twin. She looked brightly from Keegan to her husband and back again.

"I understand you tried to get your suit back from the cleaners," Keegan said to Cordwill.

Cordwill nodded.

"We have it, of course. Is there any need to tell you what we found on it?"

"Tell us, Captain," Sharon said.

Keegan read the lab report without emphasis. The blood on the suit matched that of Sylvia Lowry.

"Will you tell me how that blood got there?"

Sharon, half turned toward her husband, seemed to encourage him. But he was dully fascinated by the view from Keegan's window.

"I can't believe any of this is happening," he said slowly. "I read the papers every day. I know such things happen. But you never think you yourself could possibly get involved. . . ."

"How did the blood get on your suit?"

"I didn't notice it until I had parked downtown. I actually might have walked into my office looking like that. Thank God I did notice it. I pulled right out of the lot and came home to change."

"What time was that?" Keegan was glad he had foregone the usual stenographic record. He had a feeling that Cordwill was determined to make a Greek tragedy out of the blunders he had made.

"Midafternoon."

"Can you be more exact?"

"It might have been after three."

"It was three-thirty," Sharon said crisply. She turned to Keegan. "I had a cake in the oven. I noticed the time Bill came in."

"Three-thirty Monday afternoon." Keegan wrote on a piece of paper before him. "And you went directly from the Lowry home downtown before deciding to continue home?"

Cordwill nodded, but he did not seem to be paying close attention.

"Let's say you left the Lowry house about three. It could have been later, but let us say three. Now tell me, why had you gone there?"

"To speak with Sylvia."

"About what?"

Cordwill glanced at Sharon and she smiled.

"I am a successful man, Captain. I daresay there are not twenty men in this town who do better than I." This thought seemed to revive Cordwill and he sat erect.

"I'm sure of that."

"Good. Then when I tell you I needed money, you will understand. There are any number of ways of needing money. A poor man needs it desperately for food and shelter. A middle-class man needs it to better or sustain his position, to meet his bills. A wealthy man needs money too. He may be worth . . ." Cordwill made a suggestive arc with his hand, ". . . plenty. Nonetheless, there are times when he needs money. Cash. You must know what has been happening in the stock market during the past half year."

Keegan, who regarded Wall Street as on the same moral level as Las Vegas, who felt vaguely daredevilish depositing money in a federally insured savings and loan bank, nodded.

"Then you meant to borrow money from Mrs. Lowry?"

Put that baldly, the thought seemed to shock Cordwill. "I needed cash."

"It was hardly an ignoble thing," Sharon Cordwill said.

Keegan ignored her. "Had you ever borrowed money from your mother-in-law before?"

"Certainly not."

"This was an emergency?"

"There was some urgency, yes. Understand, I wasn't staring disaster in the face or anything near it. My problem was one of liquidity."

"Did Sylvia Lowry have a lot of cash?"

The question reduced both the Cordwills to silence.

"Naturally our investigation has acquainted us with Mrs. Lowry's recent transactions at her bank. Her banker found them unusual."

"They were. She sold off everything."

"Maybe, like yourself, she needed cash."

"Treasury notes are cash equivalents," Cordwill snapped. "How much did her bank tell you?"

Keegan recounted what he knew. The safety deposit box had indeed proved to be empty. Empty of cash. There were a few documents in it. A will.

"Then there is a will," Sharon said.

"That's what is indicated on the sealed envelope. Of course we didn't open it. Why is the will a surprise?"

"Because of what she apparently did with all the money."

"Took it home, you mean. That seems to be indicated. Tell me, Mr. Cordwill, when you went to ask Mrs. Lowry for a loan, did you imagine her just counting out the cash there in the house?"

"I don't know what I imagined. What difference does it make?"

"You thought she had nearly two hundred thousand dollars in cash there in her home, didn't you?"

Cordwill hesitated only a moment. "Yes."

"I encouraged Bill to borrow from Mother because it seemed one way to get some of the cash accounted for. What if there had been a fire?"

"Or a theft?"

"Or a theft," Cordwill agreed. "I am sure thieves have fanciful notions of what can be found lying about in the homes of those better off than themselves. But has any thief in his wildest imaginings thought a private home might have that much untraceable money sitting in it?"

"Not untraceable," Keegan said.

"Oh?"

"The bank took the precaution of issuing her new bills, in sequence, and of noting the numbers."

"Good for Bradshaw." Cordwill seemed quite sincere. "Then whoever robbed her can't use the money?"

"Let's get back to your visit to Mrs. Lowry last Monday. What time did you arrive at the house?"

"Shortly after noon."

"How long after? Five or ten minutes?"

"I left my office at eleven fifty-five. I drove directly to the house. Say I arrived at twelve ten."

"Twelve ten." Keegan wrote that down on his sheet of paper. "Did you park in the driveway?"

Cordwill cast what seemed to be a reassuring look at his wife. He seemed to have recovered completely. "I parked at the curb and walked up the driveway."

"And rang the bell."

"The front door was open. I mean the inner door. I called through the screen."

"What precisely did you call?"

"Whom, not what. I called Mrs. Lowry."

"Is that what you called? Mrs. Lowry?" Keegan cupped his hand at his mouth and mimicked a call.

"Sylvia," Cordwill corrected. "I addressed my mother-in-law by her Christian name."

"How long have you been married?"

"Twenty years," Sharon said. It seemed a round number.

"Did you call your father-in-law by his first name too?"

"What on earth difference does that make?"

"Meaning you did not."

"Very few people called August Lowry August."

"All right. You're standing at the front screen door of the house at twelve ten. You call inside to Sylvia Lowry. Once, or twice?"

Cordwill just stared.

"How many times did you say her name?"

Cordwill thought. "Twice, I think. Once quite loudly and then again. An echo call, you might say." He liked that. He was warming to the task of helping the authorities in their investigation.

"No answer?"

"No answer."

"Did you call again?"

"Yes. But first I tried the door and found it open. I went inside, calling out as I did so. I crossed the front hall to the stairs."

"Mother often stayed upstairs in her room. Praying."

"I actually started up the stairs," Cordwill said.

"And then stopped?"

"Yes."

"Why?"

"I don't know. No, I do know. It was the sound of the TV. Sylvia had a set in her sewing room, off the kitchen."

"It used to be a pantry," Sharon said.

"The television set was on?"

"That's right."

"And you assumed she must be watching it?"

"She loved soap operas," Sharon said, and her eyes misted over. "The people in those absurd dramas were as real to her as, well, as we were."

"You had to go through the kitchen to get to the sewing room?"

"Yes."

Keegan waited.

"When I came into the kitchen I found Sylvia lying on the floor, dead."

Sharon emitted a little noise and Cordwill himself shuddered.

"Where exactly was she lying?"

"Parallel to the table."

"Where was her head?"

"In the direction of the door I entered by."

"From the front hallway?"

"From the dining room. The dining room is reached from the front hall."

"Anything else?"

"What do you mean?"

"How had she fallen?"

"Face forward."

"What was the position of her feet?"

Cordwill did not understand.

"Would you say she had been coming from her sewing room?"

"No. My impression was she had come up from the basement. The basement door was open. And then I noticed the blood."

Cordwill sat back and closed his eyes. Was he seeking in the dark that scene in the Lowry kitchen? He continued to speak with his eyes closed.

"Yes. The basement door was open. She must have just come up from there."

"What did you do?"

Cordwill opened his eyes. "When I saw the blood, when I knew something violent had happened, I . . ." His voice became more measured. "I was frightened. The truth is, I was terrified. I ran back through the dining room. I actually went outside again. It's a wonder I didn't run out to my car. I wish to God I had."

"But you didn't."

"I circled the house to the back door."

"Why?"

"I've thought about that. I think I wanted to give anyone still in the house an opportunity to flee."

"Did you see a sign of someone else?"

Cordwill seemed to fight away a temptation to lie. "No."

"Go on."

"I went back into the house."

"By the back door?"

"Yes."

"So that was open too?"

Sharon Cordwill said, "Mother always locked up. She was terrified living alone, yet she did not want to give up the house. We begged her to give it up. We actually called here and asked that patrol cars keep a special eye on her house."

This was true. The request had been made a year and a half before and been renewed a year ago. Needless to say, there was not much that could be done to comply with such a request. From midnight until four, one patrol car with a single officer and a dog covered the whole quadrant of the city in which Sylvia Lowry's house stood. In any case, Sylvia Lowry had not been attacked at night.

"The doors were unlocked," Cordwill said.

"All right. You're inside the house again. What then?"

"I went through all the rooms on the first floor. Then I went upstairs. I was still frightened half to death."

"You should have called us then."

"I wish I had."

"There was no one in the house?"

Cordwill shook his head. "The basement was the worst."

"But it too was empty?"

Sharon said, "If someone had been down there, he could have left the house while Bill was upstairs."

Keegan agreed. "Very well, it is now, let us say, twelve thirty. You are in an empty house with the body of Sylvia Lowry. Did you at any time check to see if there was something you might do for her?"

The question stung Cordwill, as it was meant to do.

"There was nothing anyone could do for her."

"You could see she was dead?"

"Anyone could see that."

"How many corpses have you seen in your lifetime, Mr. Cordwill, apart from at wakes in a funeral home?"

"I served with the Marine Corps in Korea, Captain. I saw a great deal of action. We always took casualties. I have seen my share of dead bodies."

"At twelve thirty, alone in her house with the body of Sylvia Lowry, whom you saw to be dead, you did not call the police. You did not return to your office. You arrived at your own home at three thirty. What were you doing during the three-hour-long interval?"

"I stayed there in the house."

"When did you move the body?"

Cordwill's eyes closed briefly. When they opened he avoided looking at Keegan. "Almost immediately. I remembered there was a freezer chest in the basement. I went down and opened it."

"Wasn't it locked?"

"No."

"Mrs. Lowry did not keep her freezer chest locked?"

"If she locked it, she hung the key on a supporting post just next to the freezer." Sharon paused. "The only reason she locked it at all was because freezers are such hazards for children."

"Was the chest empty, Mr. Cordwill?"

"Yes. I went upstairs, picked up Sylvia, and carried her downstairs."

"Still quite sure she was dead?"

"Of course she was dead." Cordwill glared at Keegan. "What do you take me for?"

"You took Mrs. Lowry's body down to the basement and put it in the freezer chest."

Again Sharon Cordwill made an odd little sound of shock.

"Yes, I did."

"Why?"

Cordwill gazed out the window behind Keegan for a moment and then looked at his questioner. "When you say it, Captain, I still cannot believe I did it. But I did do it. It wasn't something I thought through. I just acted. I told you why I had gone to see her. I needed money. Now Sylvia was dead. I still needed money. Of course I wondered if her assailant had found the money and taken it with him, but I had to look for it myself. I could not do that with Sylvia stretched out on the kitchen floor."

"But why the freezer?"

"I don't know."

"If you were going to move her, you could have taken her upstairs to her bed. You could have laid her in the sewing room."

"Those were places I meant to search."

"But why the freezer?"

"Because it was there."

"And she would keep in the freezer? I'm sorry, Mrs. Cordwill."

"I never thought of that until later."

"Okay. So now you began to search the house for the money?"

"And I never found it. At the time I thought that very bad luck indeed."

"But now you don't?"

"You have explained that I could not have used it."

Keegan forebore asking Cordwill if he would have had any qualms about using Mrs. Lowry's money if he had found it. The question answered itself. Cordwill had not spared himself entirely. He had admitted concealing what he took to be a crime. He had admitted his intention to commit what would have technically at least been grand larceny. In Keegan's experience, anyone who admitted that much was usually concealing worse.

"Apart from your word, Mr. Cordwill, what evidence is there that you did not yourself strike Sylvia Lowry on the head?"

"I did not strike her."

"But wouldn't it be easy to alter your story slightly? Let us say Sylvia was alive and well when you arrived. You spoke of your need for money. She refused. You were enraged. There she was, an old woman with a house full of money just going to waste, not earning a penny of interest. You are determined to get it. You threaten her. She is adamant. Finally, desperate, you strike her. You are appalled by what you have done, of course; it was done in a moment of passion. Nonetheless, now the principal obstacle between you and the money is removed. You put her in the freezer and search unsuccessfully for the money. And the freezer is important. You mean to continue your search. You report your mother-in-law as missing. After you have found the money, you will place the body back in the kitchen."

"I did not strike her."

"You drove her car to O'Hare and parked it in a lot."

To Keegan's relief, Cordwill nodded. "I did need time to search the house. I did set things up so she could be reported as missing."

"How did you get back from O'Hare?"

Cordwill's eyelids fluttered. "I rented a car."

Keegan made another note. That could be checked.

"The plan came later. It sounds cold-blooded, I know, but I seemed to be moved by some madness."

"As when you took the body to the basement?"

"Yes!"

"You must have been a very nervous man when the house was being searched for clues as to where your mother-in-law might have gone."

The expression on Cordwill's face was answer enough.

"And the following day you returned to the house and resumed your search."

"No, Captain. I did." Sharon Cordwill regarded him coldly. "I searched the house. Now you see why I insisted on being here. Bill was shaken by what had happened. And of course it was necessary to get his suit cleaned. I was fully aware of our need for cash. And I had an additional motive. I did not want Jimmy to have any of the money, ever. If Mother did not destroy her will, as she once assured me she would, then Jimmy would have his share. Perhaps more than his share. One, he does not need it; two, he does not deserve it. If my mother had followed her better instincts, she would have destroyed that will and written another. Naturally, when Bill told me about Mother I was desolate. But the shock seemed to sustain me. That and the thought of the money. I have no fear of shocking you, Captain. I have no desire to impress you. I loved my mother. But she was dead. Somehow I accepted that. What Bill had done was done. The point was to go on from there."

"When did you drive the car to O'Hare?" Keegan asked Cordwill.

"I drove the car to O'Hare," Sharon said calmly.

"Is that true?"

"Yes."

"Then your husband lied."

"He was trying to keep me out of it, Captain. I think that is obvious. When Bill told me what he had done, when it was clear to me that Mother's death could go undiscovered for who knew how long, the notion that she might be thought to have taken a trip occurred to me. Very little had to be done to complete that impression. Getting the car out of the garage was an obvious necessity."

"Why didn't you take a suitcase from the closet?"

"On Monday I was unable to enter the house. After I parked the car at O'Hare, it was as though she really had gone on a trip. I pretended to myself that it was true. That made it possible for me to go into the house the following day."

"And what did you find?"

"Nothing."

"Did you look in the freezer?"

"No!"

"And you found no money?"

"I am convinced someone had already taken the money."

"Someone?"

She shrugged eloquently.

"Your brother, Dr. Lowry?"

"That is possible, of course."

"Did he know of its existence in the house?"

"You will have to ask him."

Keegan wrote on his paper, as if taking note of her advice.

"Bill did not kill my mother, Captain."

"He had motive. He had opportunity. There is a good deal of evidence, not all of it circumstantial."

"Do you intend to charge me?" Cordwill's voice shook.

"I want you to make a statement containing everything you have told me and anything else pertinent that comes to mind. When you have done that and signed it, you may go."

They seemed to grow weightless before his eyes. He detested the sense of power he felt. How easy it was to believe that these two had done away with Sylvia Lowry, yet they acted as if he had just given them absolution. Cordwill had spoken of his need for money, and Keegan believed him. The terrible thing about money is that there is never enough of it to satisfy the acquisitive instinct, no natural limit of desire for it. Perhaps even John Paul Getty had tossed and turned in his bed at night, pursued by money worries.

Keegan got up and took the Cordwills down the hall to Lieutenant Sexton. That done, he went out of the building and across the street for a cleansing glass of beer.

"IN THE front parlor," Marie said when he came downstairs.

"Mrs. Firth?" Dowling asked in a whisper.

Marie did an *orate fratres* with her hands. She did not know who the woman was either.

But of course, as soon as he saw her, Father Dowling recognized her. She got to her feet when he came into the parlor and stood silhouetted against the sunny curtains.

"We met at the funeral, Father. Mrs. Lowry's funeral."

"I remember. Please sit down."

She did, placing her purse on her knees. Her gloved hands settled on its clasp.

"I wanted to speak to you then, but the opportunity never presented itself."

Father Dowling looked receptively at Jimmy Lowry's ex-wife and said a silent prayer that he doubted would be answered.

"Would you say a Mass for Sylvia in my name?"

"Certainly."

She unsnapped her purse and drew forth a wallet. She looked a question.

"Whatever you wish."

She placed a five-dollar bill on the desk. Father Dowling put it in the drawer of the desk from which he drew forth a Mass card. He inserted the name Sylvia Lowry in the appropriate blank, signed his own name, and asked Mrs. Firth how she would like her own name entered.

"Harriet Firth."

He wrote this down, slipped the card into an envelope, and handed it to her. She seemed surprised.

"You send that to the family. To notify them that the Mass will be said."

"I don't want them to know I'm doing it."

"It doesn't matter."

"I was married to Jimmy Lowry, you know."

"So I understand."

"You don't like the past tense, do you?"

"Mrs. Firth, I know nothing of the case."

"He wanted a divorce, so I got a divorce."

Inwardly Father Dowling sighed. His earlier prayer had not been answered. "Is your present husband Catholic?"

"Are you suggesting that Jimmy was?"

"Weren't you married in the church?"

"The first time? Yes. Right here in Saint Hilary's."

"Not in your own parish?"

"I had no parish. I became a Catholic in order to marry Jimmy. Isn't that a joke? I did it only to please his mother."

"You didn't want to become a Catholic?"

"It didn't really matter to me. It was Jimmy's idea."

"You mean you felt pressured?"

"At the time? Certainly not. I was on cloud seven. Nine? Whichever. I was going to marry Dr. James Lowry of the famous Lowry family."

"Is Fox River your home town?"

"Uh uh. Peoria. I came here after two years of college. As a dental technician. I worked for Jimmy."

"And eventually he proposed?"

An expression he recognized came and went in her eyes. She thought him naïve: a priest, unworldly, innocent. If only that were so.

"We expected opposition from his parents. My becoming a Catholic was meant to cushion the blow, I suppose. But they were wonderful to me. Mr. Lowry and Sylvia. She was such a dear sweet woman and we have all been such disappointments to her. Now there was a Catholic, Father. She believed it, she lived it. I made up my mind I was going to be like her."

Dowling nodded. This poor woman must have been wanting to say these things for a long time, more urgently since Sylvia's death. Whatever version of these events she might relate to her present husband could scarcely ventilate her feelings. The Mass stipend had been her fee, buying his attention. He wished now he had not taken the five dollars, simply agreed to say the Mass. But he sent his Mass stipends on to missionary priests and it did not seem right to deprive them.

"It didn't work out?"

"It didn't work out. When I took instructions I learned

what my duties and obligations would be, and I accepted them. I fully intended to go to Mass every Sunday and not to eat meat on Friday. That's changed, of course."

"Yes. Didn't Jimmy go to Mass?"

"Rarely. Usually to impress his mother."

"And his father?"

"Even more so. If I was trying to be like Sylvia, Jimmy was trying to be like his father. He still is. That's why he gave up his practice and became such a superman of business. He had to prove to himself he could make as much money as his father had—more, if possible."

"And what happened to your marriage?"

"It's what didn't happen."

"No children?"

"He didn't want them. He made me tell Sylvia I couldn't have them, that there was something wrong inside me. And all the time we were committing mortal sin, using contraceptives. Imagine what Sylvia would have thought if she knew. In confession I told the priest about the contraception and he made me promise to stop. So I did. And I got pregnant."

Her widened eyes were swimming with tears and her lips trembled. "And I had Arthur. Arthur is retarded. Jimmy never forgave me."

He waited for her to recover. The poor woman, the poor woman.

"That was the end of our marriage. Oh, the divorce didn't come until after August died, but it was all over as soon as it became clear that Arthur . . ." She stopped and breathed deeply several times. "We put him in an institution, Father. Where he can have proper care. He doesn't know me. He doesn't know his own mother."

"Don't blame yourself."

"I don't!"

"Don't you?"

"Maybe I do. A little. Certainly the family did. Even Sylvia, I think. I mean for the divorce. Afterward I didn't see much of her. It would have been too awkward. I didn't want to see Sharon and Bill. They were furious when I came to the wake."

"That was thoughtful of you."

"No, Father. It was spiteful almost. Jimmy suggested I go, and I knew he must have had his motives."

"Jimmy!"

"Oh, I would have gone anyway. I respected and loved Sylvia. And I guess I wanted the family to see that life has treated me very well since I left Jimmy."

"Has it?"

"Yes." There was the slightest echo of regret in her voice.

"Are you worried about your marriage?"

"What's the use? I'm no longer a Catholic now. I can't be."

"Would you like me to look into that for you?" He inhaled. "For many years I worked on the Archdiocesan Marriage Tribunal. It is possible, remotely possible, that you were free to marry your present husband."

"He doesn't care."

"I wasn't thinking of him."

She did not know what to make of this. "I don't know, Father. Let me think about it."

"Certainly."

"I still do go to Mass sometimes. Not to communion. I know I can't do that."

"Think about what I said. It is only a very remote possibility. But it just might be that your marriage to Jimmy was invalid."

"Oh, it was valid all right. We had a lovely ceremony right here in Saint Hilary's. Everyone was there." Her face brightened with the memory. "The second time, well, it was just a legal thing, you know. But when I married Jimmy, believe me, it was as much of a wedding as a wedding can be."

"I'm sure it was an impressive ceremony. I was thinking of Jimmy's intent. Did he seriously mean to bind himself to you for life in matrimony?"

"If you're asking whether he would say now that he didn't, I suppose the answer is yes. Jimmy can be very accommodating."

"That isn't what I meant."

He regretted having suggested the possibility of annulment. It was so difficult to know what to say in circumstances like these. He had been moved by her nostalgia for the faith, a nostalgia no doubt fed by the death of Sylvia Lowry. If she could indeed be reinstated, if she wanted to be, he would do whatever he could to bring it about. But he feared he had given the impression that the Church is cynical with regard to her marriage laws, quite capable of bending them by denying their application. He had years of experience that told him this was not true, but would Harriet think he had suggested that with a few misrepresentations from Jimmy and herself their marriage could be declared null and void?

"Father, I did a terrible thing."

He had pushed back from the desk, considering the visit over, and her words surprised him. Was there yet another purpose of her coming here? He could not read her expression.

"Did you?"

"I've told you I admired Sylvia. I did. I wanted some memento. I telephoned Jimmy and asked him to get something for me. I suppose he thought it was a joke, what he gave me."

"What was that?"

"Her rosary."

"I see."

"He said he had taken it from her bedpost and I was welcome to it. He doubted if Sharon would know what to do with it. He gave it to me at McGinnis's, at the wake."

She opened her purse again. When she drew forth her hand and held it in front of her face, it held a rosary. A glance told Father Dowling it was not the rosary that had hung on Sylvia's bedpost. Had Jimmy played a final trick on his ex-wife?

"This isn't it," Harriet said.

"It's not?"

"That is the terrible thing. At the wake, I didn't feel right having Sylvia's rosary. It seemed more proper that it be buried with her. I switched."

The rosary she had drawn from her purse was the one McGinnis had supplied.

"How in the world did you do that without being seen?"

"Was it terribly wrong?"

"No. But I wouldn't mention it to anyone."

"I won't. It wasn't a sacrilege or anything?"

Dowling stood. The poor woman seemed aware of all the less important aspects of religion, Church rules and laws, prohibitions. Was it really her fault? Perhaps the instruction she had received had stressed the machinery of the Church without helping her see the point of the machinery.

"You must pray for Sylvia on those beads."

"I will, Father."

He walked with her to the door and went outside with her. The heat of the Midwestern summer struck them like a blow.

"A funny thing, Father."

"Yes?"

"Jimmy thought he was so shrewd telling his mother I couldn't have children. Before Arthur, I mean."

"Maybe she wasn't deceived even before."

"The joke is that it's true now. I can't have children. I had Arthur and he is the only baby I will ever have."

There seemed nothing to say to that. Dowling looked to the sky but no consoling aphorism appeared in the clouds.

"Would it still have been a sin, using contraceptives, if I really had been sterile?"

Roger Dowling squinted at the sky. What would this woman say next?

"I mean, if nothing could have happened anyway, what would we have been preventing?"

"I think you know the answer to that," he said finally.

After a moment's thought, she nodded. "I guess you're right. Thank you, Father."

She walked out to her car, a little yellow sports car, and hopped in. Roger Dowling wondered what answer it was that he thought she knew to her question. He was happy to get back inside the rectory, out of the heat.

26

ANTHONY MENDAX prowled the motel unit with its bogus French provincial furniture, yellow pine, painted and gilded, two double beds and an excess of mirrors. In them, aside from his lawyer, he saw an animal loping back and forth in his cage, dodging the lamps dangling from lightweight chains, a glass of not-your-best Scotch in his hand, completely out of sync with the self-image he had developed over the years. Out on bail, suspected of murder, more or less confined to a motel unit at the pleasure of some dimwit cop. And Foley his lawyer! Jesus Christ. What a mistake it had been to bring Foley down from Kenosha.

"This is a setup," Mendax explained to the lawyer. "I am the patsy. Now, that is your angle and you had better work it good."

Foley was not intimidated. Why should he be? Mendax already owed him too much.

"Let's not get paranoid, Tony."

The cool bastard. He seemed to think the whole fracas was only an interesting question of law. Mendax fell back on patience and logic. "Look, Foley. For once in your life, listen."

Foley gave him a fish eye.

"No, I mean it. First, I get a letter. Come to Fox River and pick up fifty thousand."

"Yes, Father Mendax."

Mendax waved this irrelevancy away. "The point is, I was being enticed, entrapped. Of course I fell for it. That is why we are here. But someone was setting me up."

"The old lady?"

"What old lady? The old lady is dead."

"*That* is why we are here."

"Foley, will you for the love of God think. Doesn't it strike you that there is too goddam much coincidence here? Isn't it convenient that I should show up just in time to take the rap for murder? Murder, Foley. Jesus."

Foley smiled. "And you didn't murder that old lady?"

"You know I didn't murder that old lady."

"So you have nothing to fear. The law, Mendax, is

sometimes a recalcitrant bitch, but in the end, over the long haul, she proves ever faithful."

"It averages out?"

"Over the long run."

Foley, who really believed this sort of bullshit, smiled a tight-lipped smile. If he did not owe him so much, Mendax would have fired him.

"The only one who saw me at that house is a priest, right?"

"The Reverend Roger Dowling."

"He's legit, is he?"

"How do you mean?"

"There really is a Father Roger Dowling?"

"There is indeed. He is the pastor of Saint Hilary's, in this city."

Mendax lifted a finger and his eyes narrowed. "But is he, the real Reverend Roger Dowling, the man who opened the door of Sylvia Lowry's house to me? Huh? Did you think of that? Maybe we are dealing with an imposter here."

"Two phony priests?"

Mendax dropped his arm. While Foley laughed, both Mendax's hands opened and closed involuntarily. Somewhere under the flab of his chins was Foley's throat, which it would have given Mendax pleasure to choke. Steady now. Cool it, Tony. I don't care what everyone says. You are not a homicidal maniac.

"It was the real Father Dowling I met?"

"Yes, Tony."

"So he is a priest."

"He is a priest."

"Can a priest testify at a murder trial, Foley? Could he put the finger on me in court? That doesn't sound right."

"Why not?"

"Because priests are supposed to be for the underdog."

Foley's mocking laughter seemed to make the hanging lamps swing on their cheap chains.

"It wouldn't look right," Mendax insisted. "It wouldn't be right."

Foley plucked more ice from the Styrofoam bucket and poured a dollop more of Scotch into his plastic glass. He settled himself as comfortably as he could on his ersatz chair.

"If you are through with fanciful theorizing, Tony, we might talk of what I learned downtown today."

Mendax, replenishing his own drink, glared hatefully at Foley in the mirror.

"I hope you told those bastards that I am heading back to Kenosha. They got their bail, what more do they want? A pound of flesh? Do they think I'm going to run?"

Foley's eyes were closed and his smile patient.

"I spoke with a Lieutenant Horvath, Tony. He is one of the detectives assigned to the death of Sylvia Lowry."

"We've met."

"Of course. I forgot. He was most informative. On instructions, I have no doubt."

"What did he tell you?"

"It turns out you are not the only one who finds it awkward to account for your whereabouts last Monday."

"I know where I was last Monday."

"But it is your little secret, isn't it?" Foley's eyes sparked with genuine anger and Mendax looked away. That was his ultimate trump, his Monday alibi, and he prayed he would never have to play it. He couldn't tell Foley now, not if his life depended on it.

"Others, I say, have a similar embarrassment."

"The relatives?"

"The relatives. Horvath tells me that a son-in-law of

the deceased has admitted to being in the house on Monday. He says he found the lady dead, carried her down to the basement, and placed her in the freezer."

Mendax stared at his lawyer in disbelief.

"He admitted that!"

"He put her in the freezer and drove her car to O'Hare. No. Correction. His wife, the daughter of the deceased, drove the car. They conspired to make what they knew to be a violent death seem merely a disappearance, a hasty trip."

"Hasn't that bonehead Keegan charged them? What the hell am I still doing under a cloud? For Christ's sake, Foley, I'm a free man."

"Not quite."

"What do you mean?"

"The couple does not admit to killing Mrs. Lowry. His story, I repeat, is that he came upon the dead body of his mother-in-law, which he then placed in the freezer."

"Why in hell did he do a thing like that?"

"The better to search the house. Mrs. Lowry was rumored to have large amounts of cash in the house."

Mendax groaned within, thinking of the fifty thousand dollars. Had she meant to hand it over in cash?

"Did the son-in-law find it?"

"That is one of the sticky questions in the investigation. The money has not turned up."

"Maybe there wasn't any."

"There had to be. She was shoveling it out of the bank; it had to go somewhere."

"They got it. The relatives. What else?"

"Now you are thinking like a policeman, Tony. We have been asked to cooperate in the investigation. As long as you are the only one charged, as long as suspicion seems to be directed at you, no matter the disrespectful way the family treated the body of Mrs. Lowry, there is the chance the money will surface."

"It can be identified?"

"It can be identified."

Mendax sat on the edge of his bed. A somewhat altered playlet played itself out in his mind. He had arrived before the murder, he had gotten the fifty thousand and gone back to Kenosha. Then the woman is killed. The money is traced to him. He shuddered. Things could clearly be a good deal worse than they were.

"Why should I help the police?"

"They will pay the expenses of your stay. Tony, it is very much in your interest that the police find out who killed that lady."

"They know who did it. If the son-in-law admits being in the house and dragging the body around, what more do they need?"

"Eventually they will go with what they have. But they want a tighter case. The money would help them a great deal."

"The guy admits searching for it, doesn't he?"

"Both he and his wife searched for it."

"I don't get it."

"If they lied about not finding the money it will be easier to convince a jury that he lied about finding Mrs. Lowry dead."

"I won't play. I'm getting out of here."

"I told them we would cooperate."

"Why the hell should I?"

"Because they have clout. Need I remind you of the irate Widow Bartley? Besides, they are prepared to proceed against you on the basis of attempted fraud."

"They won't if I stay?"

"That is the deal."

"And they're paying for this." Mendax looked about him with distaste.

Foley nodded.

"All right. All right. I have no choice."

"Well, now." Foley stood and drained his glass. "I am going to toddle back to Kenosha. Is there anything I can do for you there?"

"I'm in contact with my office."

"Good."

Foley paused at the picture window and looked out at the parking lot, sizzling in the sun.

"Where were you last Monday, Tony? What's the big secret?"

"It's not a secret."

"You just don't want to say?"

"That's right."

A moment later it was Mendax who stood at the window watching Foley wade through the heat to his air-conditioned gas guzzler. If it came to that, Mendax could prove where he had been last Monday. He had ticket stubs in his wallet. No doubt he could find the boy Willie again too, the one he had taken to the filthy flick, all-male cast, strange antics in the audience as well as on screen. Jesus, what an alibi. I was necking with a fairy in a homo theater in Chicago, Your Honor. Jesus.

27

Cheryl peered up at him through the screen door, oddly ethereal, looking as if she were composed of sun and shadow.

"Your mom and dad home, honey?"

"No."

"They're not!" He put on a desolate expression. As a dentist he had always been particularly good with kids, ho-hoing them in from the waiting room, popping them into the chair, talking a mile a minute while he gave the injection of Novocaine and the worst was over. He had never noticed the mistrustful assessment directed at him from the masks of childish panic. Nor did he perceive now that his niece did not believe his exaggerated surprise. From the window of her room she had seen his car parked up the street, facing away from the house. As soon as her parents had driven away Uncle Jimmy had made a U turn, roared up the drive, and sprinted to the door.

"I'll come in anyway," he said, turning the door handle. The door was locked. "Unlock it, Cheryl."

"What do you want?"

He laughed his grown-up laugh. "For one thing, I want to get out of the sun."

"They won't be home for hours."

"I'm going to fry right here on the step." He pretended to go limp, expecting a giggle from the other side of the screen. All he earned was the sound of the door being unlocked.

Inside, with Cheryl's assurance that Sharon and Bill would not be back for hours, he relaxed. Plenty of time. While waiting in the car he had thought of likely places to look so he would not waste his time.

"What we need is a cool drink, Cheryl. What do you have?"

"There's beer in the refrigerator."

"And what will you have?"

"I don't want anything."

"You don't have to entertain your uncle either. Look, just go on and do what you were doing. Where's Bim?"

"This isn't one of her days."

Bim was the black woman who helped Sharon with the house. He had known she was not here.

"They left you all alone?"

"I am thirteen years old, Uncle Jimmy."

"Already?"

Her stare was a little unnerving. Strange child. Well, what did he expect? It's all in the genes, isn't it? He could almost see his own father's eyes in Cheryl. He found the thought repulsive, as if a child is just a patchwork of his forebears. Grandfather's eyes, mother's chin, father's what? His phlegm, his laconic nature, his patent tolerance of James Lowry. Poor kid. Did she have any idea what a fix her dad had gotten himself into?

"I'm going upstairs, Uncle Jimmy."

"Sure. That's okay. I'll wait down here."

"They said they wouldn't be home for hours."

"I'll wait a while and then go."

He was sure he could rely on a child's inability to figure out what an adult might do. She seemed to accept the chance that her parents might return sooner instead of when they had said as reason for him to stay. She skipped up the stairs and he stood for a moment, shaking his head. Leaving a thirteen-year-old alone in the house. Strange. But no doubt Sharon and Bill were a little unglued just now. He was depending on that.

He took a bottle of beer from the refrigerator, not because he wanted it, and went through the house to the den off the living room. First, the encyclopedia. It was what he might have used himself, laying the bills between the pages. With all those volumes the set could accommodate quite a bit of cash. But the glossy pages rippled from his thumb, revealing no cache of stolen money.

They had to have it. He was convinced they did. He had gone through his mother's house with a fine-tooth comb and found nothing, and he had never as a kid had any trouble finding his mother's hiding places. The money simply was not there. Now that both Bill and Sharon admitted to having searched the house before he got a chance, he simply did not believe their story of not finding the money. Of course they had to lie. That was essential to their claim that some mysterious stranger had killed Mother before Bill got there. And what would the stranger be after, if not the money? No matter that he wouldn't have had a clue it was there, unless it was someone from the bank. Jimmy put one volume of the encyclopedia back on the shelf and removed another. The thought of the bank had given him pause. It was possible. But it was not the possibility that interested him now. He knew how much Bill had needed money. The sonofabitch had thought he could borrow from old Jimmy after the way he had acted since the divorce. How sweet it had been to plead broke, insisting on it in just the way that assured Bill would know he was lying.

"Have you asked Mother?"

"I'd rather not."

"Oh."

"I've never sought to profit from my connection with the Lowrys."

"I'm a Lowry."

"I mean before. And I'd rather she not think I'm in trouble."

"Are you?"

Bill held his breath, looking over Jimmy's head. How humbling it was for him to come hat in hand to his despised brother-in-law.

"I've tried to explain. I need money to cover a margin call. I am not facing bankruptcy."

Jimmy had shaken his head and looked dolorous. "Gosh, I wish I could help."

It was an intentionally bad line delivered as by a bad actor, something it took a pretty good actor to do. Bill was not deceived. He assembled what dignity the visit had left him and departed.

Having finished with the encyclopedia, Jimmy tried other likely volumes with similar results. The desk was next. He sat at it, put his fingers under the middle drawer, and was about to pull it open when he was aware of Cheryl standing in the doorway looking at him.

"This desk was once my father's," he said coolly. "Isn't it a beautiful piece of furniture?"

She said nothing. He pulled on the drawer. Locked. How the hell could he continue searching with Cheryl hanging around? He got to his feet. She backed away from the door. He followed her, carrying the warming bottle of beer.

"Do you know, Cheryl, I'm sorry I don't live in a house any more. Apartments are convenient in their way, but they are confining."

"Did you have a house?"

He looked at her, surprised she would not remember. But then, why should she? Did she even remember Harriet? He asked her and she nodded.

"She married again."

"I know."

"But you don't remember my house?"

"I don't think so."

"It was sort of like this one. Is there a basement?" Dumb question. She knew he knew there was a basement. "That is what I miss most, a basement."

"Grandma has a nice basement. Had," she corrected.

Dear God. He was genuinely moved. What an awful thing for Cheryl, losing her grandmother like this. He put his arm around her shoulders and felt her body stiffen.

"Don't think about it, Cheryl."

"I pray to her."

"Do you?"

"She's in heaven, isn't she?"

"That's right."

"So she must be able to see us and what we're doing. Do you think she can tell what we're thinking?"

"I don't know."

"I think she can."

"Why?"

"Because I don't talk out loud when I pray and yet she must know when I am."

"I never thought of that."

"Do you want to see the basement?"

"Let's," he said, but he was losing heart. First the thought of the banker and then the thought of Bill's broker had shaken his conviction that the money was here in the house. There were too many who had known, too many searchers.

Cheryl led the way. On the stairs, going down, she turned and looked up at him.

"We don't have a freezer."

"Neither do I," he said.

She took him on a tour of the house and it was a travesty of the search he had planned. It no longer mattered. The idea now seemed hopelessly ridiculous. What the hell did he care if Bill had gotten the money? He would have received his share eventually anyway, so was it really stealing? But it was Cheryl who had soured the plan. Talking that way about his mother, she might have been Sylvia herself, writ small, a child again, speaking in parables to her son, trying to induce in him shame at what he had become. He had meant it about the house though. He was sick of living in an apartment. He was sick of Martha too, if the truth were known.

28

HORVATH lowered his hundred and eighty-five pounds into the chair opposite Keegan's desk and opened the little notebook he insisted on carrying. As a jog to my memory, he would explain, but his memory was like a sponge. Keegan had watched him squeeze its cold water over many a defendant's case at a crucial moment, causing elation at the prosecutor's table.

"What's he been up to?"

"He had lunch at the Illinois Club, leaving his apartment at twelve five and arriving ten minutes later."

"Alone?"

"Alone. I left Phelps there to keep Martha Nagy under surveillance."

"Nagy. Is that her name?"

"We went to school together."

"What's she like?"

"A tramp. Married at eighteen, divorced at nineteen, her parents are raising the kid. Another marriage, another divorce."

"How old is she now?"

"A year older than I am."

"Thirty-two?"

"Thirty-three. I had a birthday."

"Oh." Keegan felt bad. He should remember Horvath's birthday at least. Horvath was the best cop he had.

"How long has she been living with Lowry?"

"Six, seven weeks."

"And before that?"

"Chicago."

"Doing what?"

"I told you she was a tramp."

"Any record?"

"No. But they seem to know a lot about her."

You did not have to tell Horvath what to do in order to get it done. And it was like him not to take Martha Nagy for himself but to leave her to Phelps because he had known her. Not that she would have been aware of him. He could tail his own mother without being noticed.

"So Lowry went to lunch. Then what?"

"He left at one ten, drove to Plain Street, and parked."

"Parked."

"It's down the street from the Cordwills. He parked and waited in his car."

"For what?"

"For the Cordwills to leave, I'd say. He sat there for twenty-five minutes. As soon as the Cordwills left, he made a U and turned in the drive. The daughter let him in."

Keegan thought about that. It didn't make much sense.

"He was in the house maybe forty-five minutes."

"Who was home besides the kid?"

"Nobody."

"Uncle Jimmy stops by for a visit?"

Horvath shook his head.

"What do you think?"

"The money."

"You may be right. Think he found anything?"

"No."

"Why?"

Horvath slapped his notebook on his knee, a nervous rhythm. He had a meaty face that did not reflect his intelligence.

"He wasn't as bouncy when he came out. Walked to his car. He has a habit of dashing around. He wasn't dashing. And he just drove off, no Grand Prix takeoff. He didn't get whatever it was he had gone there for."

"Then what?"

"Downtown. Bache and Company."

"Is he in the market?"

"He has an account. But it was Cordwill's he was interested in. The guy I talked to . . ." Horvath paused and something like an ironic smile formed on his great gash of a mouth. "An account executive. He was pretty insistent on the title. And he didn't like being quizzed about his customers. I told him it wasn't a quiz, just a simple question. He said I was putting him in a delicate position, just as Dr. Lowry had. Lowry had wanted information about his brother-in-law's account."

"And what did the account executive tell him?"

"Nothing. So he says. Company policy. What he didn't tell him is that Cordwill was pretty well wiped out by a margin call he couldn't meet."

"What does that mean?"

"Damned if I know. Apparently he lost his shirt."

"He said he needed money fast. Obviously he didn't get it fast enough."

"If at all."

"If at all."

Silence. Horvath was not made uncomfortable by silence. What always mystified Keegan in Horvath was the lieutenant's apparent lack of curiosity about the big picture. He did not insist on knowing how what he knew fitted in with the rest of it. Not that there was a hell of a lot he could have told Horvath about the interview with the Cordwills.

"Any idea where Lowry went from the broker?"

"The bank."

"How did you find that out?"

"Luck. I figured he didn't really have any destination, which is why I went right into Bache when he came out. Ten minutes later he was standing in front of the bank. Just standing there. Then he crossed the street to where he had parked his car. Still walking slow. So I went into the bank."

"You made inquiries?"

"I talked to Rafferty."

"Who's he?"

"The little guy who sits by the vault."

"You know him?"

"Not well. He's in my parish."

"Had Lowry been in the bank?"

"More luck. He talked to Rafferty and to no one else. I didn't ask Rafferty—it just came up. I said hello and he said how about that Lowry woman being killed, he had known her, and was I working on it. I asked why he asked. That's when he told me James Lowry had been there talking to him."

"About what?"

"Just shot the breeze, or so Rafferty thought. Lowry told him who he was. Asked if he had known his mother. Rafferty said he had. Lowry stood there, kind of moping, and Rafferty tried to cheer him up by telling him what a nice woman his mother had been. And that was it."

"Funny."

Horvath agreed.

"Any ideas?"

"Nothing that makes much sense."

"Like what?"

"Lowry wonders where his mother's money went. He knows it spent some time in his mother's safety deposit box. Rafferty is the guardian of those boxes."

"So?"

"He might have had the nutty notion that somehow Rafferty had got hold of his mother's money."

"Was this Rafferty's idea?"

"No. He thinks Dr. James Lowry is a real gentleman, stopping by like that. A man obviously mourning the tragic death of his mother and making the rounds of people who had known her. Like the Stations of the Cross."

Keegan was startled. He could not remember Horvath ever before resorting to a simile.

"Keep an eye on Lowry."

"Phelps picked him up at the apartment. He's back there."

"Did the Nagy woman ever leave?"

"No."

Horvath, having reported, left the office. Keegan rocked in his chair, his mind asea in trivia. Cordwill and his wife had given the same story in their written statement and they had been angry when he asked them to come in and go over it with him. The excuse that this was routine had not impressed Cordwill. Had he killed Sylvia Lowry? Apparently Jimmy Lowry thought so. God knows her son the dentist had spent enough time looking for the money, at her house, now at the Cordwills. And had not found it. Where the hell was it? Sooner or later someone would try to spend it, but then what? Would that give them the murderer or only one more complication?

He wished Roger Dowling had not made up that hypothesis of three different people: the killer, the man who took the body downstairs to the freezer, and the man who had brought the body up from the basement. And for "man" read "person." Granted there were three distinguishable actions, what reason was there to think they had not all been performed by William Cordwill? Keegan could not think of any reason at all. So why was he keeping that crook Mendax hanging around at city expense? He half regretted having made the deal with Foley, the lawyer from Kenosha. It would have been a satisfaction to get Mendax on fraud, or attempted fraud. Not much penalty attached to that, to be sure, but a conviction might be some protection to future victims of Anthony Mendax. Keegan could not understand people like

Mendax. Half the energy the man put into shady deals could, channeled along licit lines, make Mendax rich. He decided to keep Mendax around a little longer.

29

IT SEEMED to Keegan that Horvath was getting as bad as Roger Dowling. "Haven't we got enough suspects?"

"Cordwill said the television set was still on when he found the body."

"So she was watching TV."

Horvath did not deny this. "But the meat."

"What about it?"

"Whoever hauled it away needed a truck."

"The trunk of a car would have done."

"But whose car? Not Cordwill's. Not his wife's. Not Jimmy Lowry's. Not the car Mendax rented."

"His own car?"

"Nope."

"And you checked Mrs. Lowry's car?"

"Not a trace."

"It doesn't mean a thing."

"I'd like to have a look at Hospers' repair truck."

Keegan shook his head. "It's not a genuine lead."

"And I'd like to talk to Cordwill."

"What about?"

"Just a couple of questions about that television set."

"We are going to ask all the questions again, Horvath." Keegan looked at his watch. "In fifteen minutes the Cordwills, Jimmy Lowry, and Anthony Mendax are due here. I want you in on it. We'll go through the whole thing from A to Z. You can spell me. Unless something turns up that changes my mind, I am going to charge Cordwill."

"What does Hogan say?"

"He thinks we can get a conviction."

Horvath nodded.

"Not that he supposes the case will be tried here. There's almost certain to be a change of venue."

"But Hogan will prosecute?"

"He says he's eager to."

"I was afraid of that."

"I know, I know. But we can only do our job. Hogan has to take it from there."

He sent Horvath for a cup of coffee, a beer, whatever he wanted. Keegan had never liked this umpteenth effort to go through sworn statements in the hope that something hitherto overlooked would leap out and settle everything.

Keegan had expected his invitees to be accompanied by lawyers this time; it was the arrival of Roger Dowling that surprised him.

"Do you mind, Phil? They asked me to lunch and then begged me to come along here."

"Why should I mind?" Keegan said grumpily.

"I'll be as unobtrusive as possible. Only visible enough to provide moral support."

"To whom?"

"To the innocent."

"Thanks. I'll need it."

Dowling punched him lightly on the arm and drifted across the room to where the Cordwills were being made nervous by the rather pompous effort of their lawyer to put them at ease. The lawyer's name was Graphin; he was fifty, huge, and, as far as Keegan knew, inexperienced in criminal law. Jimmy Lowry was accompanied by Seymour Morrissey, a more logical choice, and Mendax was still in the hands of Foley.

Horvath returned and stared at the gathering. Only one who had known him as long as Keegan had could have recognized that particular version of his Slavic imperviousness as surprise.

"When do the rest of them get here?" he whispered to Keegan.

"Ha. You sit there." Keegan indicated a chair to the side of his desk, some feet from it. He hoped Horvath's position would modify somewhat the appearance his seated guests might have of a class forming a lunette in front of teacher's desk.

Keegan cleared his throat. "I think we can begin now."

Morrissey, as soon as everyone was settled, flicked his hand with the dexterity of a bidder at an auction.

"Mr. Morrissey?"

"Before we begin, I should like more clarification as to what precisely it is we are beginning to do."

"We are looking into the circumstances and causes of the death of Sylvia Lowry."

"An inquest?" The lawyer's furry brows rose like aroused caterpillars above the wire rims of his faintly tinted glasses.

"A police inquiry. I don't think we need bandy words as to why we are here. No one was forced to come. Everyone here is as anxious as I am to have this matter cleared up. I have asked you here to assist me in my task."

"Meaning," Morrissey said, "that my client can get up and go now or at any time during the proceedings with impunity and without prejudice?"

"That is right."

"An interpretation that extends, I trust, to my clients as well." Graphin seemed displeased to pin this tail on Morrissey's donkey. He was not accustomed to being outshone by a colleague and he did not like this inauspicious beginning.

Keegan nodded and looked around to make sure the ritualistic preliminaries were over. Foley held his peace, to the evident disgust of Mendax. Dowling, his chair against the far wall, sat with his arms folded, chin propped to his chest, seemingly napping already.

Keegan began. "I have constructed, from the information you and others have given us as well as from facts assembled by the detectives assigned to this case, something of a scenario of the three-day period that is of the greatest importance for determining precisely how Mrs. Sylvia Lowry met her death, the location of the body during the time when she was mistakenly thought to have gone off on an unannounced trip, and the activities of all the relevant persons during this time period. Sylvia Lowry met her death by violence. It is my duty and obligation to discover, and to charge, her murderer. I intend to meet my obligation."

Morrissey smiled unctuously. "Here? Today?"

"I have learned not to make predictions, Mr. Morrissey."

"I wondered if you were suggesting that the murderer is here in this room."

"That remains to be seen."

Graphin decided it was time to show the flag and fire a salvo or two. He moved from a seated to a standing position with a grace that made it seem a conjuror's trick, Nijinsky redivivus.

"May I object to any and all talk of murder. Murder is, I believe, a legal concept, such that the determination of a deed as murder can be made only as the result of a judicial process. I thought Captain Keegan spoke with carefully chosen words in his opening remarks. Sylvia Lowry is dead. She died, as I assume has been determined in the appropriate manner, as the result of violence. Hers was not a natural death. We are here to assist the police in their inquiry into the cause and circumstances of that death. No more, no less." He shot a glance, first at Morrissey and then at Morrissey's client. "That someone might be *accused* of murder, and arraigned on a *charge* of murder, as a result of this inquiry, to which *my* clients are happy to lend their help, is quite another matter."

"Quite," said Morrissey with a soupçon of irony.

In the back of the room Dowling opened one eye and looked at Keegan. The lid dropped again. Keegan was certain that Dowling wished he had returned to his rectory after lunch with the Cordwills.

Foley, as was inevitable now, lifted his hand for recognition.

"I fully understand," Foley drawled, "why counsel for those suspected of a crime . . ."

Bedlam. Chaos. Morrissey and Graphin vied with each other to berate Foley for his completely unethical and unprofessional remark, which, if it were not withdrawn forthwith and/or apologized for, etc. etc.

Keegan looked at Horvath. The lieutenant, who had even less stomach for such proceedings, seemed to suggest with his thoughtful look that Keegan deserved what he was getting. Anthony Mendax was enjoying himself immensely. His red plaid jacket, charcoal slacks, and white turtle neck seemed an outward sartorial sign of his inward sense of vindication. Dowling had risen and come to stand in the midst of the wranglers. His palms were displayed in a pacifying attitude.

"Please. Please. As one of the suspects myself, I have no qualms at all at being called such."

Graphin looked from the priest to Keegan. "Surely not . . ."

"What Father Dowling means will become clear if we can move on and discuss the events of the three days from the death of Mrs. Lowry to the discovery of her body. Lieutenant Horvath, would you begin by telling us what we know of the events of Monday, July twelfth?"

Horvath began at the beginning.

"The coroner puts the time of death at shortly after noon on Monday, July twelfth. It is the statement of Mr. William Cordwill that he arrived at the house shortly after noon to find the body of Mrs. Lowry lying on the kitchen floor. The position of the body, as he described it, as well as the fact that the television in the sewing room was on, suggest that Mrs. Lowry had come out of the sewing room when she was attacked. The door to the basement was open. Assuming Mrs. Lowry was dead . . ."

"She was dead," Cordwill barked, exchanging an indignant look with Graphin.

"You have mentioned the coroner's report," Graphin said. This time he remained seated as he spoke. "To what does the coroner attribute Mrs. Lowry's death?"

"She had been struck a severe blow on the side of the head." Horvath placed a large index finger just above his left eye.

"Which killed her?"

Horvath let Keegan take it from there. "The coroner thinks Mrs. Lowry died of freezing and suffocation."

Sharon Cordwill cried out. "But that isn't true! It can't be."

Graphin conferred excitedly with Cordwill. Dowling was fully attentive now.

"Is the coroner absolutely certain?" Dowling asked.

He had to repeat the question and when he had, silence fell. Everyone looked at Keegan.

"No. He is not certain. It is his opinion."

Graphin relaxed perceptibly, as did the Cordwills. Jimmy Lowry waved away Morrissey, who had seemed to want to huddle.

"Go on, Lieutenant," Keegan said.

"Assuming Mrs. Lowry was dead," Horvath continued like an interrupted tape that had been permitted to run again, "Mr. Cordwill picked up the body and took it to the basement, where he placed it in the freezer chest."

Horvath paused and Jimmy Lowry bent forward to look with disgust at his brother-in-law.

"Mr. Cordwill thought, with reason as we have found, there might be a great deal of cash in the house. He tells us his first thought was that whoever had struck Mrs. Lowry . . ."

From Jimmy Lowry came a cough that sounded like derisive laughter.

". . . had also taken the money. In any case, he determined to see if the money was still in the house. He knew this might take some time, so he decided he would arrange that Mrs. Lowry's death not become immediately known. That is why he placed the body in the freezer. Mrs. Cordwill was summoned and she drove her mother's car to O'Hare airport and left it in a parking lot there. When it was found, it did indeed make it appear that Mrs. Lowry had taken a flight from Chicago, destination unknown."

"That evening," Keegan said, taking up the narrative,

"Dr. James Lowry and a friend dined at the Cordwills. They discussed the fact that Sylvia Lowry had been liquidating investments and transferring the cash to her safety deposit box. Subsequently she removed it from the bank, apparently to her home. This was the first James Lowry had heard of this."

"How do we know that?" Graphin asked.

Jimmy gave the lawyer a bored look.

"This was the first time Mr. Cordwill had mentioned Mrs. Lowry's recent financial transactions to his brother-in-law," Keegan corrected. "After leaving the Cordwills, James Lowry and his friend . . ."

"Has this friend a name?" Foley asked.

"Her name is Martha Nagy."

"Why isn't she here?"

"That did not seem necessary."

"Did it not? If I understand what you are saying, she was in the house where the body was."

"We have taken a statement from her. Would you like me to read it?"

"Perhaps later."

"James Lowry and Miss Nagy found the Lowry home open and empty; moreover they noticed that the car was not in the garage. James Lowry called his brother-in-law to tell him this. William Cordwill telephoned me." Keegan said the last sentence flatly, but there was little doubt of what he thought of Cordwill's effort to use him in this scheme.

"The following day, Tuesday July thirteenth, Mrs. Cordwill searched the house thoroughly for most of the morning."

"And what did you find, Sharon?" Jimmy asked.

Sharon, taken aback by her brother's tone, did not answer.

"Mrs. Cordwill says she found no money in the house.

Dr. Lowry says that at no time did he search the house for money. On Monday night, immediately after calling the Cordwills, he and Miss Nagy left his mother's house. This has been corroborated," Keegan added when Graphin bent to Cordwill's whisper. "He denies returning to the house at any time prior to the discovery of the body."

"That's not true, Jimmy."

It was Sharon Cordwill.

"Mrs. Cordwill?" Keegan asked.

"I went back on Tuesday as I told you. I was sure the money must still be there. At any rate, I didn't want to give up so easily."

"You hunted around the house knowing Mother's body was stuffed in a freezer in the basement?" Jimmy seemed truly shocked.

"It wasn't stuffed," said Cordwill in an offended tone. "I realize it sounds strange, but I was very respectful of Sylvia's body."

"Of Sylvia, you mean," Jimmy snapped. "She was still alive."

"Now, wait a minute," Graphin growled, rising to his feet.

"Mrs. Cordwill," Keegan said, "you were telling us of your return to the house on Tuesday."

"Yes. As I turned the corner onto Bering Street I saw Jimmy's car pull away from the curb."

"What time was that?"

"Ten in the morning."

"Ten in the morning!" Jimmy snorted. "I'm never up at ten in the morning."

"You were that day, Jimmy. I know your car. What were you doing there?"

"I wasn't there."

"Where were you, Dr. Lowry?" Keegan asked.

"Still in bed, I imagine. What day are we talking about?"

"Tuesday, July thirteenth."

"I was still in bed at ten that morning."

"I'm afraid you weren't, Doctor. Lieutenant?"

Horvath crossed his legs and stared at his knee. "Dr. Lowry left the Crestview Building, where he lives, before nine o'clock on Tuesday, July thirteenth."

"Who says so?"

"Miss Nagy."

"I am afraid," Morrissey said, "that I must repeat a point made earlier by Mr. Foley. If constant reference is to be made to Miss Nagy, Miss Nagy should be here. I will not have my client subjected to any police tricks."

"There is no danger of that, Mr. Morrissey. Dr. Lowry, are you asking me to have Miss Nagy brought here?"

"No. No, that isn't necessary. Martha was right." He smiled ruefully, as if at the universal folly of the female sex. "Very well. I went to my mother's house on Tuesday morning. During the night I remembered what Bill had said about the money Mother had been taking from the bank. It seemed possible that she would have taken it with her on her trip, but I had no way of being sure. I had not locked the house when Martha and I left it the night before, perhaps because I thought my mother might show up at any time. The house is hers. If she wanted to leave doors unlocked, that was her right. But that seemed foolish if indeed she had money stashed around the house."

"So you went there on Tuesday morning to lock the house?"

"That's right."

"Then why didn't you?" Sharon asked. "The door was unlocked when I got there. Besides, you know it isn't true that

Mother was in the habit of leaving her house unlocked. She was frightened to death living alone."

"I thought I had set the latch," Jimmy said, unperturbed. "You say the door was open?"

"You know it was."

"In any case, you were at the house that morning. Did you go inside?"

Jimmy considered. "Yes. I checked to see if Mother had returned."

"And then left?"

"Yes."

"You were there for at least an hour."

Jimmy's aplomb deserted him, and before he could recover it his silence told against him.

Morrissey intervened. "This seems quite academic to me. My client admits being at the house. The time he spent there is quite immaterial. Even if, and of course this is an hypothesis, not an assertion, even if he had searched the house in the manner of the Cordwills, there is nothing particularly strange in *his* doing so. He had not put his mother in a freezer. He had not conspired to mislead the police as to the fact of her death. He had not driven her car to O'Hare and then misleadingly informed a police captain that his mother was missing . . ."

Morrissey's voice rose as he spoke, since Graphin was protesting the tenor and direction of these tendentious remarks emanating from a colleague he had hitherto respected.

Keegan quelled the lawyer's mock indignation. "So Dr. Lowry was mistaken in that part of his statement which he made and signed." Keegan's tone was not suggestive, but his listeners were invited to infer that one flaw in their stories suggested others. And of course Morrissey objected to that, at least as it had reference to his client.

"Summarize Tuesday," Keegan said to Horvath.

"On Tuesday the house was searched by James Lowry for one hour and by Mrs. Cordwill for several more. Once the car had been found at O'Hare, our investigation left the Lowry house free for this sort of searching." Horvath's tone changed. "Mr. Cordwill, let me ask you a question about Monday. When you found the body, the television was on in the sewing room?"

"That's true," Cordwill said defensively.

"Did you leave it on?"

"No. I turned it off. It didn't seem right, with Sylvia dead . . ."

Jimmy Lowry snorted. Anthony Mendax lit a cigarette. His interest in the narrative waxed and waned. For the most part, he was bored and made despairing gestures to Foley. Why in hell did he have to sit through this? Foley patted his knee.

"Did you notice anything strange about the set?"

"What do you mean?"

"Was it where it had always been? To your knowledge?"

"Yes, I think so. No. No, that isn't true. It was facing toward the kitchen door."

"So Mrs. Lowry could watch it from the kitchen?"

"Nooo." Cordwill closed his eyes in order to think. "No, she couldn't have seen the screen from the kitchen table. Or from the sink. Not from anywhere in the kitchen really, except from the doorway itself."

"Was the set far into the sewing room?"

"Yes."

"Was it pulled away from the wall?"

"What are you getting at?"

"I am trying to find out the placement of the television set."

Keegan permitted Horvath this indulgence. He looked

toward the back of the room and was surprised to see how interested Dowling was in this turn of the discussion. Keegan tried to figure out what significance the television set made. Unsuccessfully. It seemed more prudent to align himself with Horvath's intuitions.

"You said the set was far inside the sewing room, Mr. Cordwill. How far inside?"

"Three quarters of the way."

"Are you sure?"

"Yes. I think so."

"Am I to understand that Mr. Cordwill is an expert on the placement of the furniture in the Lowry home?" Morrissey asked.

"Thank you," Horvath said to Cordwill and dropped the subject.

Keegan took over. "Later on Tuesday, after he had said his Mass at noon, Father Roger Dowling went to the Lowry house."

"Why?" Jimmy Lowry turned to look at Dowling.

"Simple curiosity, I'm afraid."

"Did you search the house too, Father?"

Dowling nodded and Jimmy turned to Keegan.

"And the police, naturally, have also been through the house?"

"Of course."

"Looking for clues?"

"For clues," Keegan agreed. "Which includes the money, if that is what interests you. We did not find any money."

"Nobody found any money, "Jimmy said slowly. He looked at his brother-in-law. "Now, why do you suppose that was, Bill? Unless the money was no longer there."

"Jimmy!" Sharon said. "Don't be silly. We spent hours looking for it."

"*You* did, yes. Maybe Bill didn't tell you everything."

The Cordwills sat back in their chairs, disgusted with Jimmy, but he had managed to put the worm of doubt into his sister's mind.

"While Father Dowling was in the house, Mr. Anthony Mendax called. He was wearing clerical clothing and introduced himself as Father Winter."

"I nearly said Father Christmas," Mendax piped, but no one thought it funny.

"Wasn't that description unnecessary?" Foley asked sadly. "Whether Mr. Mendax called dressed as an Eskimo, a priest, or a Tollhouse cookie is neither here nor there."

"His clerical clothes were explained," Keegan continued, "by a letter Mrs. Lowry had written him. One of Mr. Mendax's companies publishes religious tracts and pamphlets. Mrs. Lowry had been much impressed by one of these pamphlets and, thinking Mr. Mendax's company was an enterprise of a religious order, she wrote offering to donate a sum of money in return for prayers for her late husband."

"How much?" Jimmy Lowry.

"Fifty thousand dollars."

"Did you get it?" Lowry asked Mendax. Foley prevented his client from responding, but gave his own head a negative shake.

"Father Dowling asked Mr. Mendax in and the two chatted. Father Dowling told Mr. Mendax that Mrs. Lowry was not home and had apparently gone away."

"Whereupon Mr. Mendax left," Jimmy carried on, parodying Keegan in a singsong voice. Then, in his natural voice, he said, "Did you check this man's story?"

"Charges were brought against Mr. Mendax."

"And have now been dropped?"

"That is right."

Jimmy shook his head.

"Father Dowling left shortly after Mr. Mendax," Keegan concluded. "That is pretty much the story of Tuesday, July thirteenth.

"The following day, Wednesday the fourteenth, at nine thirty in the morning, we received a call. An anonymous call. The caller said Sylvia Lowry is in her kitchen. The body was discovered ten minutes later."

"Where?" Foley asked.

"On the kitchen floor."

Morrissey asked, "Where precisely on the floor?"

"Facing the sewing room."

"Not facing away?"

"No," Jimmy said.

"How would you have known?" Bill Cordwill asked Jimmy bitterly.

"On Tuesday, in midafternoon, Dr. James Lowry again visited his mother's house."

"What is this?" Jimmy protested. "And don't tell me Martha told you that."

"No," Keegan said. This was the biggest gamble thus far. "Mrs. Harriet Firth."

The Cordwills became agitated.

"Oh God," Jimmy groaned. "She wanted a souvenir. She was ashamed of herself for marrying again, ashamed because it had stopped her from seeing my mother. She idolized my mother. She had heard that my mother had withdrawn from us, the children, and she felt responsible. I told her she wasn't. When she heard my mother was missing, she phoned and we talked. It set her mind going. Other things, better days." There was a wistful tone in his voice. "She wondered if I would give her something of Mother's."

"Of all the nerve."

"Something small and inexpensive, Sharon. A memento. Don't be so goddam greedy."

"It is your generosity that amazes me. Why would you be distributing Mother's things if you thought she was still alive?"

All eyes were on Jimmy.

"I didn't think it would do any harm."

"And what did you give her?"

Jimmy smiled with venomous sweetness at Sharon. "A rosary. Something I was sure you wouldn't want."

"Mrs. Firth confirms the gift of the rosary," Keegan said. "It was at that time, on Tuesday midafternoon, that James Lowry carried his mother's body up from the basement."

Morrissey had been sitting on the edge of his chair, waiting for this.

"Hold it there. When the body was found by the police the following morning, was it in a frozen condition?"

"No. It had thawed."

Sharon Cordwill shivered and her husband put his arm about her shoulders.

"And you could compute from its condition how many hours it had been since it was taken from the freezer?"

"Yes."

"Is it not that fact, rather than anything Mrs. Firth told you, that underlies the extraordinary accusation you have just made against my client? Aren't you guessing? Aren't we faced here with the sort of police trickery I mentioned earlier?"

But Jimmy Lowry, smiling, put his hand on Morrissey's arm. "I did it. I did it. It doesn't matter, Sy." He turned from his lawyer and looked at the Cordwills. "Can you imagine what it was like, opening that freezer and finding Mother in it? You bastard, Bill. I knew it was you."

Graphin began to speak, but Jimmy glared him down.

"What I don't get, Captain, is how the hell the police could search the house and not find the body."

"A good question," Keegan said.

Horvath nodded. "Of course we weren't looking for a body. But even so . . ."

"In any case, we now know how the body got upstairs again. Dr. Lowry should have called us as soon as he made his discovery and not waited for whatever reason until the following day. Both removals of the body were highly irregular and complicated what might otherwise have been a relatively simple matter. However, it is the first removal that is the more serious. The man who was there at a time close to the death of Mrs. Lowry and who hid her body is also the prime suspect for administering the blow to Mrs. Lowry's head. Mr. Graphin, I am charging your client, William Cordwill, with murder in the second degree. I think that is all."

Bill Cordwill rose spluttering to his feet. "I didn't do it."

"We will make our defense in court," Graphin said. At the moment, he wanted to stop Cordwill from saying anything more.

The room emptied quickly. Jimmy Lowry and Morrissey were outside before Graphin cornered Keegan at his desk. Anthony Mendax, having told Foley to run on without him, went to where Roger Dowling still sat in his chair at the back of the room. The priest's eyes were closed and his arms were folded across his chest.

"Reveille," Mendax said, touching Dowling's shoulder.

The priest smiled sheepishly and got to his feet.

"I'm on my way, Father. It was a pleasure to meet you."

Dowling took the outstretched hand.

"Father, I am going to send you, gratis, a supply of pamphlets for your church. To prove I bear you no ill will."

"That is very kind of you."

"Anthony Mendax looks to the future, not to the past."

"Good luck to you."

"Same to you, Father." Mendax patted Dowling on the arm and clattered from the room on high wooden-heeled shoes.

"Father?" It was Sharon Cordwill, her face twisted in worry. "Father, how can we stop them? Bill didn't murder my mother."

"I know."

"You do?"

"The case is circumstantial, no matter how damning it looks at first glance. I don't think Bill has much to worry about."

"You said you knew Bill did not kill Mother."

"He did not murder her," Dowling said carefully.

Sharon rushed back to Keegan's desk. Horvath, who was waiting patiently for Cordwill and Graphin, came up to the priest.

"Some mysteries remain, Lieutenant."

Horvath nodded. "The meat."

Graphin had turned away from Keegan, his expression professionally fierce, but he could scarcely be surprised that he had failed to change Keegan's mind. Horvath took the Cordwills and their lawyer from the room. Keegan emitted a long sigh.

"Thanks for telling Mrs. Cordwill that her husband is innocent, Roger."

"I told her he had not committed murder."

"Why don't we let a jury decide?"

"I was not thinking of what a jury can decide."

"You seemed interested when Horvath got going on Mrs. Lowry's television set."

Dowling did not hesitate. "I found the whole thing

interesting, Phil. You must be exhausted. Would you like to have dinner, courtesy of Mrs. Murkin and the parish of Saint Hilary?"

"Not tonight, Roger. I want to be fresh as a daisy when I talk to Hogan in the morning." He rose and his frown deepened. "Hogan and Morton both."

"Two Achilles' heels," Dowling murmured.

"You can say that again," Keegan growled.

30

"WHO CALLED?" Gene Hospers asked. "Mrs. Murkin?"

"No. Father Dowling. It's his set."

"What's wrong with it?"

"He didn't say, Gene. Why would he tell me?"

"People always say what's wrong with their sets. The first ten minutes of a call I spend listening to them telling me what's wrong with their set."

"Well, he didn't say. What do you care? It's a job, isn't it?"

"I looked at his set the other day, when I was there working on Mrs. Murkin's."

"It's funny, a priest watching TV."

"What's funny about it?"

"I don't know. You know. I mean, does he watch the shows we watch or what? I'll bet he watches Channel Two."

Edna Hospers made a face. Watching Channel Two was her idea of a lenten penance. In the front room their own set was blaring, some goddam game show, but at least it fascinated the kids. Gene Hospers himself rarely watched television. All day long he had a set going inches from his nose, but he never paid much attention to what was on it.

"You going to call?" Edna asked.

"Call who?"

"Father Dowling."

"What the hell would I call him for? I can't fix a set over the phone."

"Well, don't get mad at me. I don't see what you're so mad about anyway."

"I'm not mad."

"You act as if we don't need the money."

"We need the money."

He finished lunch, yelled good-by to the kids, waited for an answer and didn't get one, blew a kiss at Edna.

"What time you want supper?"

"Who knows?"

"Call me."

He got into his truck and drove to his shop, where he called Omar Pearson, a competitor.

"Omar? Gene Hospers. Say, I'm going to throw a little business your way. Sure I'm serious. I'm up to here and can't make the call. Yeah. I don't know. Just says there's something wrong with his set. Okay. Guy named Dowling. That's right. Father Dowling at Saint Hilary's. Okay? Fine. Don't tell him I called you. Just say you're there about the TV. Hell no it's not a joke. What do you think I am? No. No. Look, my shop is full of jobs that are overdue. Goddam it, if you don't want the job, say so. All right. Yeah. Dowling. Saint Hilary's. That's okay. You're welcome. You can do me a favor sometime."

Hospers put the phone down. God, what a suspicious bastard Pearson was. Oh, maybe not. It did sound kind of funny.

It was funny, Dowling calling him like that, calling his home when he couldn't reach him at the shop. What the hell was he trying to pull?

Gene Hospers fooled around a bit with a Hong Kong radio some sucker had bought from a discount house. Fixing it would cost a lot more than it had been discounted, a lot more than the damned thing was worth. But he couldn't concentrate. He hadn't worked, really worked, for over a week. He was jumpy, what else, though he had convinced himself there was no reason to be. The newspaper had been full of it at first, but there hadn't been a story for days. They had hauled in some guy from Wisconsin and that had set off the talk again, but now that too had subsided. He shouldn't be jumpy, but he was.

His conscience? It didn't help much to laugh aloud at the thought. It wasn't the money. Maybe it was a mortal sin to take that much money, but Gene Hospers could not really think so. He remembered discussions in grade school: how much money do you have to steal before it is no longer a venial sin, but serious, mortal, killing the divine life in your soul? Five dollars? More? Even as a kid he had thought it was ridiculous. Was $4.99 okay and $5.01 a mortal sin? Money didn't really matter much. Mortal sin meant sex, sex and murder.

He actually shuddered. If Dowling hadn't made such a big deal out of the money, he would have gone on and told him the whole story. It didn't matter what the paper said, murder and all that garbage. You had to be involved in something like that to know how innocent it could be. He had only wanted to shut her up. He had begged her to shut up. He had offered to put her goddam steak back in the freezer if it meant so much to her. But she grabbed at the package and pulled at his shirt and he couldn't get away from her to go down in the basement and put the meat back in the box. Did he even mean to hit her when he swung? Hadn't he just been trying to get free of her?

Funny, the more you played back a scene like that, the more confusing it became. You began to doubt your memory. And if he himself wasn't sure what had happened, how could anyone else be? He had swung his arm, still holding the frozen meat, and she dropped to the floor without a sound. He beat it out of the house then. Of course he had known, after his first theft, why she was so excited about the package he had taken from her freezer. And now he had another. He did not start the motor of his truck and get out of there. Why run? She would blow the whistle on him and there wasn't anywhere to run. Better to clear it up right now. My God, he had to think of Edna and the kids.

But when he went inside and saw her still lying on the floor of the kitchen, when he bent over her and saw what had happened, all panic left him. His problem was solved. A pretty cold-blooded thought, maybe, but he had really felt relieved. He actually started to say a little prayer of thanksgiving before he could stop himself. And then he thought of all those other packages in the freezer. It was a helluva hiding place, you had to give the old girl credit. And he was the only one who knew her secret.

Had it taken him even ten minutes to get the contents of the freezer into his truck? When he pulled out of the driveway and into the street he could have sung out, he was so glad to be out of there, free and clear.

And not one single package had contained anything other than meat. He couldn't believe it. He had parked in an alley on the west side and opened every goddam package and there was nothing but chops and roasts and steaks and ground round. Into a trash can it had gone, all of it; what could he do with that much meat, how could he explain it to Edna? That had been the hardest part, not talking with anyone. He simply could not tell Edna.

Going to confession had seemed to provide a safe chance to tell someone about it. You could tell a priest anything and he couldn't breathe a word. And Gene Hospers had wanted absolution too. He wanted it even more than the psychological relief of talking to someone about what had happened. Unbelievable. It wasn't exactly guilt he felt. How could he feel guilty when the days went by and there wasn't a word in the paper? He began to doubt it had really happened. Was he going off his nut? So he had gone to St. Hilary's and rung the bell by the confessional. When he heard Dowling coming he piled into the box, ready to go.

Strange he should be asked so soon afterward to look at the housekeeper's set. And then when he came out of the rectory kitchen and saw Dowling on the stairs, he knew the priest knew he was the one. Just knew it. And now another call. Psychological warfare? Hospers grinned, but the grin faded. Dowling couldn't talk. Not even now, when he had connected what had been said in the confessional with Gene Hospers and Sylvia Lowry. That was the connection Gene Hospers had seen in Dowling's eyes when he came out of the rectory kitchen and faced the priest.

Maybe Dowling thought he could get him to talk about it outside the box, when a priest was not bound by the seal of the confessional. Well, if that was his idea, he was going to be disappointed. Let him figure that out when Omar

Pearson showed up at the rectory. Nobody was going to outfox Gene Hospers, at least not easily.

It would be different if he felt guilty, if his conscience really troubled him. He assured himself it did not. His conscience was clear. No one could convince him that taking money from someone as rich as Mrs. Lowry was a mortal sin. As for hitting her, okay, he had hit her. But what the hell, he had hit Edna. Once he had struck his own mother. Had he meant to kill Edna or his mother? Certainly not. Well, that is the way it had been with Mrs. Lowry. If he ever did go to confession and say he had killed her, that would be a lie, and there was a serious sin for you, lying in the confessional.

Besides, look where they had found the body finally. At first he couldn't believe it. He read the story half a dozen times. He listened closely when Edna babbled about the horrible news. He couldn't have forgotten doing something like that. He never could have done it. It was the deed of some kind of ghoul, a creep. Imagine, a nice old woman like that. Gene Hospers shook his head. The kind of nuts running around loose you just wouldn't believe.

Someone had come into the shop. Hospers called out, to let whoever it was know he was in back. A great big guy was waiting in the front for him, looking at the secondhand sets Gene had been trying to sell for over a year.

"You Hospers?"

"That's right."

The man took out his wallet and opened it. "Lieutenant Horvath. I'd like to ask you some questions."

"Don't I know you?"

Horvath stood there waiting for Gene to decide if he did.

"Where did you go to school?" Hospers asked.

"Saint Cyril's."

"Sure. You played baseball for them."

"Did you play for Saint Hilary's?"

"You remember me?"

"No."

"I played right field." It was the traditional position for the ungifted athlete.

"How'd you get into TV work?"

"Don't ask. I guess I had the aptitude. It's not so bad."

"Just repair?"

"I sell a few rebuilts. Not many. Who wants a second-hand television?"

"They work?"

"Sure they work. They're black and white."

"I don't have a color set."

"Too bad."

Horvath looked at him impassively.

"Color sets are the best thing ever happened to guys like me. Your hundred-dollar black and white lasted forever. The picture tube went eventually but it was maybe the first trouble you had. And how much is a picture tube? You know what they want for a color set, even a portable?"

"I know."

"And repairs? You wouldn't believe it."

Horvath nodded. "You ever work on a set belonged to Sylvia Lowry?"

"Is that your first question?"

"That's it."

"And you know the answer. I put a little sticker back of any set I work on, with my name and phone number."

"What was wrong with her set?"

"Which time?"

"You hear what happened to her?"

Hospers looked sad and shook his head. "Why did he do it?"

"Who?"

"The guy you arrested."

"Maybe he didn't do it."

In junior high Hospers had been in a play and in one scene he was supposed to register surprise. The director had insisted that he turn slowly toward the audience while letting his arms move away from his body, flex his knees and move his blank-faced stare slowly thirty degrees from left to right. He had brought the house down. It was supposed to be a serious scene and the director was madder than hell. For years afterward, guys would say, Hey Gene, look amazed. And he would move his body, lift his arms, bend his knees and stare stupidly into space as his head moved from left to right. All that came back to him as he realized how he had reacted to Horvath's remark.

"You mean that?"

"When was the last time you were at Mrs. Lowry's?"

"Is it important?"

"Who knows? Maybe you saw something."

"Or somebody?"

"When was it?"

"Let me think." He thought for a while, in pantomime.

"You keep any kind of records?"

"A place this small?"

"No copies of bills?"

Hospers snapped his fingers. "Wait a minute."

But Horvath came with him into the back room. His pink copies of bills were in a box on top of his desk. Nervousness left him when he realized there would be no bill for the day he struck Mrs. Lowry. He found two others and handed them to Horvath.

"This is the most recent one?" Horvath waved one of the bills.

"What's the date?"

"April twenty-first."

"That sounds about right."

"Anyone else ever work on her set?"

Hospers looked baffled.

"Can you tell if another repairman has been working on a set?"

"Sometimes. Not always."

"How about Mrs. Lowry's?"

"Nooo, I don't think so. At least not before the last time I was there. In April."

"That your truck out back?"

His name was all over the side of the truck.

"Yeah."

Horvath handed back the pink copies and Gene went with him through the shop and out front.

"Thanks," Horvath said.

"That all?"

"Do you know anything you think would be helpful?"

"I wish I did."

Horvath turned away. "Thanks again."

"That's okay, Lieutenant."

He watched the cop get into his car and drive away. Inside again, he let out a howl. Honest to God, it was better than confession talking to that dumb cop. And he had hit just the right tone, he was sure of it. No crocodile tears for his poor dead customer, no big curiosity when Horvath suggested they didn't know who did it. The alarming thought he had had at first, that Dowling had put Horvath onto him, had dissolved when he remembered that Omar Pearson should have been at the rectory now, working on the priest's set. It did not matter that Dowling had made the connection. The seal of the confessional would keep him quiet.

Horvath was just a thorough cop. He had noticed the

sticker on the back of Mrs. Lowry's set, made a note of it and followed the lead. Which had taken him nowhere. The name of Gene Hospers would now have a line drawn through it in Lieutenant Horvath's little book.

31

KEEGAN came for supper the following evening. He seemed glad to have his own involvement in the death of Sylvia Lowry behind him, a matter of record.

"No doubt Hogan will foul up the prosecution." Keegan's lips were flecked with beer foam. "But that is his concern, not mine."

"Graphin, or whoever defends Cordwill, is going to be grateful for Morton's testimony."

"Who knows? Morton may make up his mind what killed Sylvia Lowry by the time Cordwill goes to trial."

"Perhaps."

Keegan looked woefully at the TV. Did he perhaps wonder why he was so loyal to a losing team?

"Cordwill did it, Roger. He put her in that freezer without knowing for certain she was dead. How could he? He's no doctor. She might have been revived if he had called an ambulance. He killed her."

Dowling nodded. "Yes. He killed her."

"Then why in hell did you tell his wife he didn't? I mean, I can understand consoling a parishioner, but that was going a little far."

"I meant it, Phil. Cordwill did not murder Sylvia Lowry."

"Maybe not legally, if you mean first degree."

"I wasn't thinking legally," Dowling said softly.

Keegan, about to answer, seemed to understand and did not.

The following day Gene Hospers deposited two thousand dollars in his account at the Fox River Savings and Loan. Two one-thousand-dollar bills. Their serial numbers indicated they were from among those issued to Sylvia Lowry by her bank when she sold her Treasury certificates for cash. Lieutenant Horvath immediately impounded Hospers' repair truck so the lab could go over it. He did not arrest Gene Hospers.

"The police have been here asking for Gene," Edna Hospers told Dowling in a desperate whisper. Her children were down for their naps.

"I know. They asked me to come here."

"What in the name of heaven is going on?"

"Where is Gene?"

"I thought he was at work."

"He isn't."

"That's what the police said. He must be out on a job."

Dowling shook his head. The Hospers' living room seemed a replica of one of those ads in a Sunday supplement whose colors transgressed the borders of the pictured objects, a roomful of furniture for $298, the epitome of ill-constructed bad taste. Perhaps, given the destructiveness of the Hospers children, it didn't matter.

"They found his truck at the shop, Edna."

Her surprise was less excited now. She sat, stunned,

staring at the floor where a patch of sun lay despairingly on the synthetic fibers of the carpet.

"The police asked for the license number of our car. They won't tell me why they want Gene."

"You've no idea why?"

"No." But conviction gave way to doubt. "He's been different lately, Father. He seemed less worried."

Dowling had not expected the remark.

"About money, for example. He used to grouse about it so. And with reason. The shop is such an up-and-down affair."

The vivacious Edna Hospers Father Dowling had known was now a confused and frightened young mother. It was impossible not to pity her and the poor little tots sleeping upstairs.

"You mustn't worry." He seemed to have an endless supply of idiotic remarks.

"Thank you for coming, Father."

But he had shamed her with his knowledge of her trouble, whatever it was. He could not tell her. It seemed wrong that the police had not.

After saying Mass at noon, he had lunch and then went upstairs to his room for forty winks, but he could not sleep. The air conditioner complained against the heat, his room seemed an oppressive place, cut off by its coolness and the hum of that motor from the wider world. His mind was full of the death of Sylvia Lowry. It was impossible not to think of what he knew and could not reveal. Where had Hospers gone? The man seemed a symbol of us all, prowling the earth, heavy with his sins, no doubt still deluded that his crime had gone undetected. But it was his sin rather than his crime that made Gene Hospers symbolic for Roger Dowling.

He turned off the air conditioner and went downstairs to his study. Marie was baking cookies and the aroma filled the house. Father Dowling read listlessly Canto Nineteen of *Il Purgatorio* and then, as always, became absorbed. Dante expressed the only concepts of reward and punishment Dowling could feel comfortable with. He studied the Doré ilustrations of the covetous, whose punishment was to be chained face downward, turned to the earth, their backs to heaven, their condition in purgatory symbolizing what their lives had been.

He was interrupted by the signal from the church indicating that someone wanted to make his confession. It was as an interruption that he responded to it, going irritably to the door and into the heat. But between the rectory and the church he found again his sense of values. How could it be considered an interruption when a priest was called to the work of a priest?

The penitent was already in the box. Dowling could hear a restless stirring while he got settled in his chair. He paused a moment to murmur a prayer and then slid back the panel. He could smell liquor before the man spoke.

"Bless me, Father, for I have sinned."

Recognizing Gene Hospers' voice, Dowling involuntarily straightened in his chair. Whether because he noticed the priest's reaction or not, Hospers did not go on. He breathed heavily on the other side of the grille, his breath thick with alcohol.

"Yes?"

"I committed adultery."

"Has this happened before?"

A pause. "Yes."

"With the same woman?"

"No."

"Do you know her well? Will you see her again?"

"No. No. It was a girl I picked up in a bar in Chicago."

"Are you truly sorry for offending God in this way?"

"Yes."

"It is also an offense against your wife. You have broken trust with her."

"You told them, didn't you?"

Hospers' tone was no longer that of penitent to priest. His face seemed to be pressed against the grille.

"When I got back from Chicago, I phoned home. Edna said you had been there. What are you, a priest or a cop?"

Dowling was almost relieved that Hospers had revealed himself.

"We should talk about this somewhere else. This is not a confession."

"Ha. You'd like that, wouldn't you? No, this is a confession. We are here and I am telling you my sins."

"Very well. Then tell them all."

"So you can tell your friends on the force?"

"I have not betrayed your confidence. Please believe me. And I know you do believe me. You indicate as much by insisting we remain in the confessional."

"And you were trying to trick me into talking outside."

"I would like to help you. You have stolen a great deal of money. This is already known. The money you deposited in the bank was traceable to Sylvia Lowry."

Hospers inhaled at the mention of the name.

"And you know what happened to her, don't you?"

But Hospers did not speak. There was only the sound of his breathing, shallow, apprehensive.

"You struck her when she surprised you stealing the money."

"It wasn't money." Hospers' voice was odd, as if he were sharing a joke. "It was *steak*."

"You struck her with a package from the freezer."

"I didn't mean to hurt her. I didn't mean to hit her. She was clawing at me, trying to take away the package." Hospers spoke in an urgent whisper and Dowling could sense the anguish in the man's voice.

"You must tell the police what happened."

"No!"

"Another man has been arrested."

"But you must have read what he did. He put her in the freezer."

"But you had struck her down. That may have been what killed her."

"I didn't want to. I didn't murder her."

After a moment Dowling nodded, though he doubted Hospers could see this. "No, perhaps not. Your sin was not murder."

"Sin! It was steak. Lousy steak. That's all I stole. Only one package contained money and I got that the first time, by accident. You see, when I did steal money, I didn't mean to, and when I meant to, all I got was steak."

Was it possible that Sylvia Lowry's death had come to this, a repairman's theft of steak from her freezer? Of course it was possible. He had no right to doubt Hospers.

"Very well. Now let us make this confession a profitable one for you. You have confessed a sin of the flesh. You confess to intending to steal some money. And, in striking Mrs. Lowry, you had no intention to harm her, to kill her? Is that right?"

"It is, Father. Honest to God."

"And you will return the money? When you confessed that earlier, I told you you must return it."

"Yes!"

Dowling drew in his breath. "All right. I am going to give you absolution. But before I do, let me give you some advice. As soon as you leave this confessional, telephone the police. It will go much easier with you if you tell them just what you have told me."

"They won't believe me."

"You're wrong."

"You've got to help me, Father. They'll listen to you."

Dowling could not refuse. Besides the return of the money, he told Hospers he must say the rosary for Sylvia Lowry every day for a week. Hospers agreed eagerly. And then, as he recited the formula of absolution, Father Dowling felt his sense of the irony of this situation leave him. How often the deed we mean to do turns into something else, something we did not really intend. A relatively innocent action, an instinctive response, can look to the outsider like a criminal deed. It was that outsider's vantage point that Phil Keegan must adopt, but it was different in the world of the confessional, where the Divine Comedy was somewhat less enigmatic and more mysterious. A priest learns how frequently truly sinful deeds can wear an innocent public face. The outward consequences, the observable effects of what we do are seldom commensurable with the true nature of our acts.

When they left the confessional, they stood for a few moments as if surprised to see the other there. This was a unique sequel to an exchange in the privacy of the confessional.

"Come with me," Dowling said. "You can use the telephone in the rectory."

When they arrived at his study, Hospers asked Dowling to make the call, but he was finally convinced it would be better if he did it himself.

"Ask for Captain Keegan."

Hospers dialed and asked for Phil and waited nervously for a full minute before saying, "Hello. Captain Keegan?

This is Gene Hospers. I'm at Saint Hilary's rectory. Yes. Yes, I know. He's here with me. Okay. I'll wait here. I'll be here."

He hung up the phone and looked to Father Dowling as if for praise.

"After they come, I'll go speak to Edna."

It was then that the full consequence of his phone call dawned on Hospers. His mouth trembled. He nodded and sat down.

When the doorbell rang, Dowling let Marie answer it. The sight of Keegan did not surprise her.

"He's with someone just now, Captain."

"Send him in, Marie," Dowling called.

Keegan stood in the doorway and looked from Dowling to Hospers. If he was curious about what had led up to this scene, he managed not to show it.

"We'll have to go downtown," he said to Hospers.

"Right."

"There is no need for you to say anything until you are represented by counsel," Keegan said dutifully.

Hospers, on his feet, nodded.

"I've got nothing to hide."

Keegan stepped back to let Hospers precede him from the room. He looked reproachfully at his old friend.

"Mrs. Lowry's television set," he whispered.

"Lieutenant Horvath is a very shrewd man."

"Yeah. I'll call you."

"What was that all about?" Marie asked when the front door had slammed.

Dowling looked at his housekeeper, a wise old widow whose curiosity had not been dimmed by thirty-five years of rectory life.

"That," he said, "is a very long story."

32

A WEEK later the Cubs, who had been ahead by seven runs at the end of the fifth, were tied in the sixth and finally beaten in the thirteenth. Dowling was glad to turn off the set.

"Another beer?" he asked Keegan.

"I don't think so."

"The Cubs always lose, Phil. You should know that by now."

"It isn't that. More of the money showed up. In Chicago."

Dowling, thinking of Gene Hospers' day of dalliance in the big city, nodded.

"Over a hundred thousand."

Dowling lurched.

"Fotion Jewelers. A small concern."

"How on earth . . ."

"All perfectly legitimate too. Sylvia Lowry was buying diamonds."

"Where neither moth nor rust consume," Dowling mused.

"And do you know what she had done with them? Get this. She had Fotion replace the Our Father beads of her rosary with diamonds. She was saying her prayers on a rosary worth over a hundred grand."

"The family must be relieved."

"There's more."

"Oh?"

"Her will. She made an addition to it. She left that rosary to you. To Saint Hilary's parish, to be exact."

This was true. Eventually a rosary was brought to Dowling by Mr. Graphin. The lawyer was somewhat ceremonial in making the presentation. Dowling signed a paper acknowledging receipt on behalf of St. Hilary's parish; Graphin put the paper into his briefcase and became less formal.

"An odd thing about those beads, Father Dowling. James Lowry had given them to his ex-wife as a memento. I got them back by exchanging a rather handsome crucifix that had hung on Mrs. Lowry's bedroom wall. Of course I did not explain why it was imperative to get the rosary."

"I'm grateful."

"You will want to have the stones appraised of course."

Dowling said something noncommittal. Graphin was not the sort of man who would appreciate what had happened. Neither, it turned out, was Phil Keegan.

"They're just glass beads?"

"It is at best a three-dollar rosary."

"They slipped you the wrong beads?"

He assured Keegan that that was not it at all. He explained then what had happened and the story emerged, because of the delight he had taken in anticipating its telling, as a polished vignette. To his disappointment, Phil's reaction was anger, at Jimmy Lowry, at Harriet Firth, at Sylvia too. But then perhaps allowances had to be made, given what had happened to Keegan's cases against Bill Cordwill and against Gene Hospers. It turned out to be as impossible to prove that Hospers' blow had killed Sylvia Lowry as it was to convince a jury that Cordwill's putting her into the freezer had ended her life. Morton, the delphic coroner, thought either possibility equally likely.

"The ass is telling me that because I have two murderers I don't have any."

"Or that you have no murder."

"A woman was killed, Father. Society cannot be maintained if things like that go unpunished."

"Society is built on unpunished crimes."

"You don't believe that."

"Oh, but I do."

Keegan had shaken his head in exasperation. Of course this would not affect their friendship. It was important to Keegan's view of the priesthood that Roger Dowling be somewhat naïve and unworldly.

But his tolerance did not extend to the rosary. Two days later he handed the exhumed treasure to Dowling.

"Oh, no! I wish you hadn't done that."

"I did it for the parish. You need the money. So does Desmond."

Dowling shook his head sadly. "And I have been praying that she would rest in peace."

"I did it. You didn't."

"They look like glass to me." Dowling held the jeweled rosary up to the light. Well, Sylvia had meant for St. Hilary's to have it.

"You got a safe place to keep that?"

"You mean somewhere moth and rust do not consume nor thief break in and steal?"

"I need a beer," Keegan said, and huffed from the study.

Roger Dowling put the rosary in the drawer of his desk. Thank you, Sylvia, he thought. Now, may you rest in peace.